A New Orleans Virgin & A Hood Millionaire

Miss Jazzie

A New Orleans Virgin & A Hood Millionaire

Published in the United States of America.

Published by Cole Hart Signature, LLC.

Mailing List

To stay up to date on new releases, plus get information on contests, sneak peeks, and more,

Go To The Website Below...

www.colehartsignature.com

Dedication

God, for without you I am nothing. You give your hardest battles to your strongest people. Thanks.

Yhental

"I'm getting up now Ma, damn," I yelled through the door, saying the latter to myself.

My mother, Yhena, was on the other side of the door yelling, "Class starts at 9. Don't make me kick down this door and beat yo' ass." She tried her best to cuss but couldn't because her Japanese accent wouldn't let her. Her telling me what time class started was not going to make me move any faster. I hated when she tried to wake me up like I was still in fucking high school. I knew what time my class started.

"Well I don't hear you moving around in there!" she yelled again, beating on the door. This time I whipped the cover from my body, flipping my middle finger to the door as if she could see it. I got out of bed and stomped to the bathroom for a quick shower. Yhena was a deep pain in my ass. She was always stern and punctual with me and my education but when it came to my brother, he could torch a fucking building and she would provide the gasoline. Sometimes I felt like she loved him more because all she did was show affection to him and fuss at me every chance she got. If it wasn't my clothes, it was my hair, and I was tired of that shit. My brother caused all types of mayhem in the New Orleans streets but all he got was a pat on the back from her or maybe she just ignored the shit. Maybe her stupidity came from her Japanese heritage. I wish she would loosen the leash just a little bit, because her being all in my mix made me want to leave New Orleans for good.

I did everything she requested of me. Graduated high school as valedictorian, receiving a full scholarship to Xavier University where I was a pharmacy major. My graduation party was three weeks away but everything else was a surprise. I knew my father was gon' do it big for me just like he did for BJ when he graduated, or even bigger because I was his baby girl and nothing was spared when it came to me. After begging and pleading with her and plus my father taking up for me, I was granted permission to take a year off before heading to pharmacy school at Spelman. If the decision was up to just my mother, she would have had a fucking stroke. She felt like if I took a break then I wouldn't finish, but that was a lie. My dream was to become a pharmacist, and nobody but God could change my passion.

I kept everything intact, including my hymen. I didn't even live the typical fast ass life of a girl that was twenty-one. I had to beg my mom to let me pledge Delta Sigma Theta. Bakari, my dad, was all for it because he wanted me into some extracurriculars, and it was the best feeling I'd ever had. Nhairobe, my best friend, and I pledged together so we were really sisters. We were in the trenches and crossed over together. I could only participate in the step shows but couldn't go to any of the pledge parties because I didn't live on campus. I started to wonder if my mom would ever take me off the tittie, but the older I got the harder she was pushing me away from her and made me want to rebel. I loved my mother, but I didn't like her. I respected her, but I didn't like that she always made decisions for me.

I only had one class and that shit was about to be over because I was going to take the test early so I wouldn't have to complete the class. All I had to do was wait for graduation. I knew I would pass because it was a pharmaceutical class that I had been studying for, for the past two weeks. I thought about telling Yhena but decided against it because I knew she was gon' make up more shit for me to do and I wanted to enjoy life, even if was for a few weeks. The only people who knew were BJ and Nhairobe, because she was taking the test too. Yhena would get mad as fuck when I went to Bakari when she said no because I knew it was a definite yes, except for the parties. He was overbearing to an extent. If I wasn't studying, I was reading. I only had one friend, Nhairobe, or Nay Nay as I like to call her. She'd been my friend since elementary school, but we were like vinegar and oil. My girl liked to party but because of my overbearing maw, I couldn't do shit. I wanted to go to parties and live life, but she always had some shit for me to do or read. I mastered education but was a dummy to the streets.

"I'm up, Ma, get away from my door!" I yelled from my private bathroom letting my accent slip out.

Yhena was Japanese and met my father, Bakari, while he was in Japan on some type of business. Till this very day, I didn't know what type of business a New Orleans nigga had in another country, but whatever. A hood nigga from New Orleans in Japan? Yeah, okay. I never questioned it because I never got in grown folks business. From what I know, they had a whirlwind romance, and my mother became pregnant with my brother. Of course, her people didn't approve of it, but my mother chose my daddy and she left with him to come to the states. Before my brother was born, my daddy married my mother and she gave birth to him in New Orleans. Fast forward five years and I came. I was a daddy's girl to the bone gristle. A bitch couldn't tell me nothing about Big Bakari and vice versa. He owned my entire heart outside my brother. BJ was my boy-best friend. I could see how my daddy had my mother smitten. He was a charmer, and his loyalty ran deep. My parents had been married for almost 27 years. I wanted a love like theirs, if my mother ever let me kiss a nigga. I wasn't allowed to go to the mall without one of my father's men with me. Even when Nay Nay was with me my father's men weren't too far behind.

"Leave that girl alone, Becky, she grown as fuck," I heard my daddy calling my mother by his little nickname for her. A smile graced my face at him defending me. "Let her do her and you go find yoself some fucking business, like riding this dick." I could imagine my mother's face turning beet red at his words as I heard his voice fade. That was the norm for him to talk to her like that and deep down, I believed she liked that shit. I turned the shower on full blast, ready to get my day started.

I grabbed my scrunchy and put my hair in a messy bun because I knew the steam from the hot water would have it back to its natural curly state. That's another thing Yhena hated. She always wanted my hair straight like her hair was, but I'm glad it's curly. That's my lick back for her being a thorn in my fucking side. Because of my father's African American heritage and my mother's Japanese background, I was considered blackanese, or at least that's what the girls in the hood called me when me and my girl went through St. Thomas or St. Bernard. If my father knew that shit, he would kill me. My hair was crazy thick though. I always went to the Dominicans and had them straighten it, but it wouldn't last a week before it was curly all over again. Sometimes I would let Nhairobe straighten it, but it was so long this bitch started charging me. I didn't mind though, because it was a job. My wide hips, thick thighs, and apple bottom had to come from my aunts on my daddy side because my mother was flat as a pancake. She had a little ass, but for the most part she was a damn bean pole. I knew I inherited her slanted gray eyes and hair because we practically looked like twins except body wise. I had a nice set of C-cup breasts that didn't sag, with a button nose and full pink lips. That paired with naturally arched eyebrows and long eyelashes gave me an exotic but innocent look. I thought my mother would have loosened the rope around my entire life, but it didn't matter how much my daddy fussed with her, she stayed on my ass about everything.

I was twenty-one years old and still lived with my parents. I loved the fact that it was rent free, and it was a compound, but I begged my daddy for me to get my own place and he always declined, saying I wasn't ready for that. BJ had his own shit and he was 26, but his ugly ass still had keys to the house. He came and went whenever he wanted to. It was so bad that my brother or father brought me to school every day since elementary. That shit was so embarrassing. I had to practically beg him to buy me the Camaro that I currently had with the help of BJ, but I could only drive it to school and back and sometimes on the weekend when I wanted. I couldn't live on campus because Yhena didn't trust me, and Big Bakari said he had too many enemies for me to even think about living on campus. What the fuck did his enemies have to do with me? BJ got to run the streets with his hoes that I'm sure my father knew about, but I was stuck in the house like a caged fucking bird.

I couldn't reflect too long or Yhena would bust in my room to see what was taking me so long to get ready for school like I was a fucking child. I just prayed that I was able to take my own car that had been collecting dust in the garage. I hopped out the tub and grabbed my towel to wrap around my body. It was 6 a.m., way too early for me to be woke, but I knew we were having breakfast as a family. I quickly dried myself and walked in my walk-in closet and pulled out my black Chanel romper with the matching signature slides. I wanted to be comfortable today, plus me and my girl were going to the mall after the test. We deserved a shopping spree and it didn't matter who was buying. I opened my door and the first boisterous voice I heard was BJ.

"Ye, bring yo' ass down here before the food gets cold! You know Dad ain't letting us touch the food until his princess makes her presence known." He was being sarcastic but honest. My daddy would stop the world for me. I walked slowly down the stairs on purpose just because I knew he was probably starving because he never cooked. His hungry ass didn't miss a meal when my mother cooked. One by one, I walked down the spiral staircase until I hit the last step. All eyes were on me, but my disgusting ass brother was the first to speak, yet again.

"The fuck you think you going with that short ass shit on? All yo' ass hanging out, and since when you started wearing make-up?" he barked at me, causing a scowl to grace my face.

"First of all, I don't wear makeup, and if I did!? It's my damn face and I'mma grown woman. I make my own choices. You starting to act like yo' parents." I rolled my eyes to the ceiling because my momma already had me pissed off waking up early for this dumbass breakfast, and here he was with his dumb shit.

"Yo' ass got on lashes and everything. That shit them dust buckets from the St. Thomas be wearing. Don't think my niggas from the east didn't see you and Nay messy ass walking through there probably to cop some gas, and don't say it wasn't you because I got the fucking pictures in my fucking phone! Didn't I tell you to stay out the fucking hood, Yhental!?" he yelled and cussed at me with no regard for our parents being there, and they didn't say shit.

"First of all, I don't smoke fucking weed! We went through there because Mrs. Tay has the best cold cups, and you know that because you used to take me before you got so heavy with this street shit with Daddy and the Melph Monstas that you forgot about the little shit we used to do, so don't watch me and what I do," I yelled back at him with evil intent in my eyes. His friends all reported my whereabouts to him. He was worse than Big Bakari and I was over it. He looked at me and shook his head, then my father chimed in like this was a three-way call.

"I know y'all motherfuckers grown and shit, but the level of respect still remains intact when y'all in my fucking house. Respect my shit and watch y'all mouth," his voice roared like thunder, trying to shake the fucking table. They had officially fucked up my appetite and I wasn't hungry anymore.

"Ye, baby, you might wanna to change clothes because I don't approve of it either. The bottom is too short and your ass cheeks are damn near spilling out the bottom. You are not going to school like that." He tried to calm his voice and reason with me, but I wasn't budging.

"Why? Because BJ said so? Daddy, you never checked what I wore to school and you saw me every morning, so what changed?" I asked him because it was true. He never asked me to changed my clothes and I have worn worse shit than this. BJ was on some bullshit too because he never questioned what I wore or where I went. He was usually on my side and blocking shit so my daddy wouldn't see or know shit.

"No, because I said so. If you haven't noticed, yo' hips spreading and your body is changing. I would hate to have to have a nigga head leaking for looking at my daughter. You have all type of shit in that closet that you could wear," he continued his rant, but I had something for his ass. He was showing off in front of BJ, but I would beat him at his own game.

"So if I go change my clothes to your liking, can I take my car instead of somebody bringing me? Fair exchange means no robberies, right?" I cocked my head to side and smirked. I noticed BJ behind him with steam coming from his ears. I looked back at my daddy with puppy dog eyes. He stared at me hard for a few moments before giving me his angry stare that I never fell victim too. I used his own words against him when he wanted me to do chores around this big ass house.

Yes, Ye, you can take your car to school, and here." I watched as he reached in his back pocket and pulled out a small envelope. I opened it and revealed a black Amex card with my name on it.

"Happy graduation, Ye." He then reached in his other pocket and handed me my key fob to my car. "Enjoy your day Ye, you deserve it, but after you change your clothes." I didn't give him a chance to get the rest of his words out before I jumped on my daddy, raining kisses all over his face. I enjoyed his laughter in my ear, and I looked behind him and poked my tongue out at my momma and BJ because I knew they were salty.

"Girl, get yo' heavy ass off me before I change my mind," he laughed as I unwrapped my legs from around his waist. I may have been a grown woman, but I was never too grown to be my daddy's girl. I landed on my feet as we sat down to eat breakfast.

BJ kept cutting his eyes at me like I was a baby, and I laughed because he knew I would get my way. I rushed to eat and went back to my room to change into my clothes but with a twist. This time I put on a pair of black skinny leg jeans that sat right on my waist with a black V-neck T-shirt with Armani exchange written in white across my breasts. That with a pair of black Jordan's completed my outfit. I grabbed my stuff and headed out the door, bypassing my family because I knew they would have something to say again.

Bakari Jr

"That's why she is the way she is now, because of you. If Momma says no then that should be the end of it, but you always overlook Moms," I told Big B as we cleared the table. I watched Ye rush out the door, and my mother went to the living room to probably catch up on her soap operas.

"Don't come talking yo' shit like you haven't handed over a couple of your own mistakes, Bakari," he said, calling me by my government name. Any other time I was Tonka because of my size, but today I was raggedy ass Bakari. "All the bitches you came to me about abortion money that ya momma still don't know about, so don't come in here trying to run my fucking house, nigga. You got yo' share of secrets too," he said low enough so just he and I could hear.

He was right. I did fuck up a lot and I didn't know why. I was lucky to walk away without an STD because I didn't believe in using protection. I was a daredevil, but the bitches made it so easy for me to get the pussy. All I had to do was walk through a room and the kitty was being thrown at me. It could have been because of my looks or being my father's son, but I never turned it down. Sometimes I used protection then other times the pussy was too good to use it. I got checked every six months so I knew I was clean. Unlike Ye, who got her slanted eyes and face from Yhena, I was the splitting image of my father. From his cognac-colored eyes and dark mocha skin to his solid built physique. People would think we worked out on a regular but I hated the gym. I only went to let off steam in the weight room or run the treadmill, both of which I had in my home. At 6'4 with dreads that touched the middle of my back, the ladies' panties melted at the first sight of me, especially the hood bitches. I even entertained the thought of letting Ye buck me up to get a skunk stripe like her ass like we were twins. The only difference is mine was platinum. I kept telling her that we weren't twins, but the puppy dogs eyes got me every time. My father was ready for me to settle down, but I wanted a woman who wanted me for my mind, not what I could offer her or my reputation.

"You right, Pops, I been fucking up a lot lately, but I'm good now. I been keeping my dick in my pants until the right one comes along, then I'll settle down and head for the brass ring, but these hood bitches latch onto me like maggots to shit," I told him, and he laughed.

"Yea, you been fucking up, but you know I got yo' back just like I got Ye's back," he told me, and I agreed, but he was a little too hard on her so I decided to speak on it to see his reasoning. We heard footsteps coming down the steps and knew it was Ye's nosey ass, so I waited for her to leave. She bounced by us wearing too tight jeans and a shirt that was tied so tight that her belly button was showing, but my dad didn't notice. Before I could say anything, Ye left out the door.

I turned to my father and asked, "You got everything set up for the meeting?" It was time for our quarterly meetings with the rest of the Melph Monstas. It was time to see what the count was and who the fuck we had to pull up on to get the rest of the money.

"Yeah, ya mommy out for the next couple hours trying to figure out what the fuck they saying on the TV." I laughed because my mother had been in New Orleans long as I'd been alive and she still didn't know the English language that well. Bakari offered her to take classes and even Rosetta Stone but she refused, saying that she didn't need a program to teach her shit. I must admit her shit was better than it was when we were growing up, because we had to point to shit for her to know what we were saying. Now she could say lil' shit here and there that we understood. By me and Yhental being born here, Pops taught us everything we knew from English to Japanese so we could communicate with her, but she got mad when we spoke to her in Japanese. Shit crazy, right? But all we could do was respect it.

"I got my man cave set up for all the lieutenants. Them niggas ate already before they got here so no need for extra food, and I wasn't trying to feed them anyway," Pops said as we headed to the basement.

When we walked in everyone stopped talking. I stood on the left side of Big B as we stared at them. We had seven lieutenants that were in charge of the seven parishes in the state. They each had five men that worked under them that went to different ports to get the shipments of drugs and guns to bring back to the city. They then were distributed and paid for and each lieutenant was responsible for bringing their cut to our monthly meetings. I could tell by the look on Juju's face that his shit wasn't straight, but I didn't say anything. Piper smiled as we made eye contact because I knew he had his money. The rest of them niggas knew what would happen if they were short, so they just nodded their heads up and down. Piper was my right hand. He was the only nigga I trusted outside of my father with my life. When shit went left, he made shit right.

"I brought you men down here to speak with you all privately but still collect my money," my father said, and I looked confused because he didn't discuss the details about this meeting other than collecting the money and going our separate ways. "As you men know, I have been running the Melph Monstas for the past twenty-five years. I have had a good run and now it's time for me to step down. I'm getting tired of the day to day but I still will be in the background." He looked at me and winked his eye with a smirk. "Bakari Jr, or Mello as you all call him, will be taking my place and I trust that he will choose his right-hand man wisely." I didn't wanna show emotion, but I was happy as a hooker with a bunch of dicks. I stood stoned face, looking at each of the men in their faces. Me and Piper were the youngest and most ruthless of the crew. I knew tables was gon' shake at the gesture and change in position that my father just made.

"This is my last drop as your boss. Moving forward, everything will go through Bakari," he said and nodded his head toward me. He looked toward the men and nodded his head, which meant it was time to pay up. One by one, they stepped in front of my father and dropped Louis Vuitton duffel bags filled with money at his feet and walked away. Juju was the last to step up, but he didn't drop his bag.

"The fuck is the problem, nigga?" my father barked at him.

"I'm ten bands short because my nigga from the Magnolia was short, but I'll get the rest, boss." He stumbled over his words. I watched my father watch him and knew shit was about to get bad.

"That sounds like a you problem, nigga. Where is the rest of my fucking money," he said calmly, but I knew the storm was coming. "Why the fuck would you even attend this fucking meeting if you didn't have all my money, nigga?" He unfolded his arms and walked closer into Juju's personal space.

"Cuz, nigga, I didn't want you to come and hunt me down." And he would be correct, because when niggas were late with the money, me and Piper went on a prowl and took the money. It didn't matter what territory got trampled on or who got killed in the process.

"You would be fucking right. At least you honest, so what the fuck you gon' do about it?" I intervened, and my father smirked. I stood in place rocking from left to right, because if he was short then my family didn't eat, and I had a problem with that.

"I'mma get you the money but I need like a week, Mello," he called me called me by nickname. My father gave me that nickname as a kid because of my calm yet deadly demeanor. I watched Piper walk behind him, silently putting him in a choke hole. I pulled my switchblade out my back pocket and walked over to him. I was about to chop the tips of all ten of his fingers off for every band he didn't have, but my father stopped me.

"Never shit where you sleep, Mello. This nigga got 48 hours to run me my fucking money or you can handle your business. Let him go, Piper," my dad stated and walked out the basement door, leaving the three of us.

"Bitch, you better get the rest of my money or it won't be your fingertips I cut off, it'll be your throat that I fucking slit," I barked at his butch ass as Piper pushed him toward the steps, and he stumbled up them. When we heard the door close, we both started laughing. I got serious and looked at him.

"Nigga, you ready for this?" I asked him, keeping eye contact.

"I was born to do this shit, nigga, but my real question is, are you ready to fill those big ass shoes?" He reversed the question back to me.

"I ain't filling my father's shoes because I can fit my own. He stepping down. It's my throne now." I dapped him off as we left the basement to part ways.

After I chopped it up with my pops and made sure that I had somebody on Ye, I headed to a freak I was fucking on named Tasha. She was from the St. Thomas and I ran through her every now and then because her head was off the meat rack. She was fine lil' redbone who was a nurse at University Hospital. She was perfect for me, no kids, own apartment and car, educated, sexy as fuck with hazel eyes, and independent. The only shit that got to me was the fact that she didn't want to leave the hood. I was from the hood, even a product of it ,but we didn't stay long. My father owned a compound in Eastover, but I had a condo in Downtown New Orleans. I felt like I was too old to still be living my parents. I never brought bitches to my parents' home and the same went for my shit. You had to be wifey to see where I laid my head at because I didn't trust nobody. Piper didn't even know where I lived and he'd been my nigga since the sandbox days.

I pulled up to her apartment and hopped out. All the bitches were looking because I was the nigga to fuck with. Although shit wasn't official between me and Tasha, I would never disrespect her by fucking a bitch in the same hood she lived in. She carried herself like a lady but behind closed doors, she was my hoe. I swagged to her front door and twisted the doorknob because I knew it was open. She knew I was coming and what I was coming for. I turned to make sure I locked it before I made my way to my destination. I walked through her small living room that was decorated in all shades of pink. I went down the hallway and opened her room door and I heard her moans. I looked toward her bed, and there she was with her pink lingerie getup on with her legs spread wide and fingers deep inside her tunnel. My dick got brick through my jeans. Her pussy was sloppy wet and I couldn't wait to dive in. Let me clear some shit up for y'all though. I wasn't about to eat her pussy, but my dick was about to sink deep in her guts. Yeah, she a nurse and shit and I knew she kept herself clean, but I didn't eat pussy. I never did and probably never would. Every bitch I came across knew I wasn't gon' eat the pussy and if they even mentioned it, I put my dick up and it was over. I ain't even eat fish and wasn't about to start.

"Damn, you couldn't wait for me?" I groaned as I pulled my dick out through my jeans.

"No, you were taking too long," she moaned as I watched her pussy glisten as she circled her clit. I began to jack my dick as felt the precum leak out the tip and hit the floor.

"You got me making a mess and shit on your rug. What you gon' do about it?" I asked her and removed her hands from her clit. She got on all fours and crawled over to me, and I watched her ass jiggle from the front as her wide hips made their way to me. The tip of her tongue licked my dick and I hissed.

"You know I got you." And that she did. She gobbled my shit. My entire dick went straight down her throat, no gag. She deep throated my shit and massaged my balls, sending me into a sexual frenzy. She had a nigga weak behind her mouth.

"Hmmm," she hummed, and my head fell back. My hands went to her lace front as I guided her up and down my shaft. Her tongue slithered like a snake each time my shit hit the back of her throat, causing it to wet up my balls. My hands touched the net that held her wig together, and I almost snatched that bitch off and threw it across the room. She must've been reading my mind because she stopped momentarily.

"Don't think about it Mello, I just got this lace front installed and I actually like this one. Don't pull it off," she said and went back to sucking my dick.

"I paid for this one and I'll pay for it to get done again the fuck, stop playing with me," I moaned as she went faster up and down my dick. She suctioned her cheeks and cupped my balls, putting it all in her mouth, and that was all I could take. I gripped her wig and snatched that bitch off and flung it to the wall. Even the fucking net came off and her braided hair displayed going down her back. That's what I didn't understand. Tasha had long ass hair but wanted to wear other people's shit.

"Fuck that wig, Tash, I got you. Get up and bend that ass over," I told her before she could even get mad. "I don't even know why you wear that shit when you got your own hair." I smacked her ass and watched it move like the ocean. I went in my pocket and grabbed a Magnum and rolled it down my dick. I slapped my shit on her ass as she twerked, giving me a show. Her hazel eyes met mine as she licked her bottom lip.

"Stop playing and put that dick in me, Mello," she said, and I slid inside her and fucked her fast and deep. Her pussy squeezed my dick and I was ready to bust.

"Fuck girl, what type of spell you trying to put on a nigga?" I asked as she threw that ass back.

"Ain't no spell nigga, this pussy good as fuck." She circled her hips, making me nut. She kept fucking me while my nut seeped into the condom, until I was too tired to stand and fell over on her bed. I tried to regulate my breathing but after that nut, I thought I was about to have a fucking heart attack.

"You good?" she asked me as she removed the condom to flush it. I watched her ass move as she disappeared into her bathroom. I ain't have to worry about her saving a nigga's nut because she didn't want kids and I didn't either. I heard the toilet flush and she walked out with a soapy towel. She took my jeans and boxers off and cleaned my dick and balls. Nursing was her passion. I could tell by the way she took care of me when I came through. She always made sure I ate, had a good nut, and left her a happy man. In return, anything she asked me for, I gave willingly. That was our situation, no strings attached, but we knew what it was.

"You hungry?" she asked me, breaking my thoughts. She threw on her nightgown and laid beside me. She knew that was a no-no. Soon as her head hit the pillow beside me, I sat up to put my jeans and boxers on.

"You don't gotta go because I laid down Mello, my legs hurt," she said, and I knew it was a lie. She wanted to pillow talk and I didn't do that shit because that's where feelings got involved.

"Nah, I'm good, I gotta head out anyway. I got some shit to do," I told her without looking back. I knew if I looked back this conversation would go somewhere that would end up with her crying and me cursing her ass out.

"Damn, I'm good enough to fuck but we can't even have a conversation Mello? That's how it is now?" See what the fuck I mean. She got soft every time I fucked her. I think it was time for me to move on.

"Nah, it ain't like that, but I already know how the shit gon' go. You want some shit from me that I'm not giving you. It ain't that you don't deserve it, but I ain't the nigga to give you that. I be trying to spare yo' feelings, but it's like you want a nigga to hurt you and that's not what I'm trying to do, but you trying me," I told her the truth, and she hated that.

"Well damn, tell me how you really feel. You know I want more from you, but where I live and where I'm from don't define who I am as a woman." Now she was giving attitude that I didn't have time for. I had a bad ass temper and she'd witnessed it before and ended up with her table being broken in half and bruises around her neck.

"I always tell you how I really feel and you can't handle it. You wanna throw lamps and shit and fuck up your own furniture that I have to replace every time. Why not take the easy way out and take us for what we are and let shit be. If you can't handle it, let me know and we can end this shit now with no hard feelings," I told her straight up because ain't no sense in lying. I knew what Tasha wanted. She wanted the fairytale ending, marriage and a house with the white picket fence and unicorns and shit. I was a fucking bull and would remain that way until I met a woman strong enough to tame me, and it wasn't Tasha. She thought she could change me and I always told her that I could and would only change if I made that decision. She couldn't make it for me. She was too soft and controlling, and I didn't need a bitch clocking my moves.

"Whatever Mello, I know I said I could deal with what we had, but I want to be the woman you settle down with when or if you ever decide to," she said, but my back was still to her.

"That's the choice you're making to wait for me, because I'm not asking you to. All I ask is if you start fucking with another nigga, let me know so I can move accordingly because I don't wanna step on the next nigga toes." I knew I was being harsh, but it was honest.

"That's the thing Mello, I wanna be with you. There is no other nigga," she told me, and something inside of me believed her.

"You need to get you another nigga to get all your attention off of me then," I told her as I slipped into my tennis shoes.

"So you telling me you fucking other bitches?" she asked me, and I laughed. I didn't mean to but she was asking some shit that she knew would fuck her head up.

"Do you want yo' feelings hurt?" I asked her and finally turned my head to face her.

"Just tell me the truth, Mello," she said, her voice cracking. I don't know why she set herself up every time, but she wanted to know so I was about to be as real as I could be with her.

"You know you not the only female I'm fucking with. I'm a single man so I owe no one an explanation as to who I'm fucking and not fucking. That's the whole point in me not settling down. I'm not trying to hurt you in any way, but you asking me shit that you know the answer will hurt you. What we doing is what we do, and that is all it will ever be, Tasha," I told her, and the tears started to roll down her cheeks. That's why I didn't want to tell her shit because it always ended up like this.

"Get the fuck out my house Mello, witcho dog ass. I knew I shouldn't have let you in this time because it always ends the same fucking way. Money ain't everything. I don't ask you to buy me half the shit you buy me, but that's your own guilt for fucking over me." She got hysterical and I knew shit was about to start flying across the room, so it was time for me to leave.

"Guilty? For fucking over you? How can I fuck over you when we not together? That's where you get shit fucked up at. I give you money and buy you shit because you cool as fuck and don't get all emotional, but now I see that was a big mistake. Let me get the fuck outta here before I really hurt yo' feelings, Tasha," I told her and stood from the bed.

"My friend told me you was a dog ass nigga. She said you would hurt my feelings and that I shouldn't fuck with you because you didn't give a fuck about people," she yelled at my back as I walked out her room. I turned to her as she stood from the bed with a sheet wrapped around her body. She was such a pretty woman but not the woman for me.

"Well, you should have listened to your fucking friend then. That's probably the same friend that wanted to fuck me and got mad because I didn't, but she was right. I am a dog ass nigga and I ain't fucking with you no more." I walked out her room, but before I made it to the door I could hear shit crashing against the wall and her screaming shit I could barely make out. I went to her refrigerator to grab me a bottle water while she did all that, then I went out her front door. I was officially done with Tasha and everything about her. I would send Piper back over later with a few bands to buy the shit she broke in her room.

I hopped back in my car and headed in the direction of the blocks that Juju ran, although I knew I shouldn't have, but I knew the nigga that shortcut him and he was about to pay up. Just like I had a family to take care of so did Juju, and he shouldn't have to come out his personal money because his nigga was short. I pulled up and got out my car with my gun in my hands. There was a bunch of niggas shooting dice on the side of the corner store. Hunnids on the ground as they stood around talking shit. One of them noticed me and stood up, and it was like the domino effect because they all got quiet and stood to their feet. I was only there for one motherfucker, and that was the one looking at me like he'd seen a ghost. That nigga looked like he wanted to shit himself because he knew I was coming for him.

"Nook, let me holla at you right quick." The niggas around him parted like the Red Sea because they heard of me and what the fuck I was capable of. I watched as this nigga walked to me with his head down. "Pick ya head up, nigga," I barked at his ass, and he lifted his eyes to mine. I stepped to him, taking in every nigga that was with him just in case one of them wanted some smoke.

"Is this why the fuck Juju was ten bands off with his fucking count? Because you wanna shoot dice and lose yo' fucking money when you should be fucking working?" I kept my voice low so only he could hear me. "Just like you answer to him, he gotta fucking answer to me, and when he didn't have my fucking money, what the fuck you think gon' happen to him then you?" I asked him, and he acted like he couldn't talk. I rarely made street calls, but this shit was personal because I felt like this lil' nigga was playing with my money. I watched as his ass shook like a fucking leaf but tried to keep it together because he was in front of his boys.

"Nah, this ain't that. I was short because—" I didn't give him a chance to get anything else out before he heard my fucking gun cock.

"I don't give a fuck what it is. When the fucking money is due, I expect all of it. You supposed to be running the fucking block, but you out here shooting fucking dice like you ain't got shit to do with the homies. Clear this shit out and get back to the fucking money before I air this bitch out and take this block back. Matter of fact, that money on the ground is mine, go pick my shit up," I told him, and he looked at me funny.

"That's they money. I just got in on the game. I can't fuck with they money like that," he said, and I chuckled.

"You really think I give a fuck whose money it is? I said fucking get it. Now clear this out and get back to the fucking money. If you don't have my bands in the next 48 hours, I'mma make yo' entire fucking family dance. Nah go get my fucking money, nigga." I hit him in the mouth with the butt of my gun. That lil' nigga was strong because he didn't stumble. He held his face as it gushed with blood. He went back over to his people and whispered some shit I didn't hear. I noticed everybody picking up the money and then going into their pockets and get whatever money they had. They each one by one walked over to me and gave me what they had and I gladly took it. All I would do was give it to Ye and her friend to spend at the mall later. After everybody gave me their money, I looked at Nook.

"I'll see you in 48 hours." I saluted him and walked back to my car and hopped in. I ain't have to worry about nobody playing with me because I ran the fucking streets and everybody in it.

Nhairobe

I swear I hated living in the Magnolia project, but it was all I knew and was comfortable with. I was a product of rape. My mother was raped at sixteen and didn't abort me. However, right before I left out the door to attend my high school graduation, I went back in the house thinking she was behind me and she wasn't. I walked further in the apartment, stopping in my room to spray perfume on me. I'd called out to her but she didn't answer, which was crazy because she'd just helped me put on my cap and gown. There was a limo waiting for us courtesy of my girl Yhental and her fine ass brother, so we were straight. I walked into the small bathroom and my beautiful mother was hanging from the ceiling fan. I knew my mother suffered from depression because of the rape and often said she regretted keeping me because I looked just like the man who raped her. I never knew the man and she never volunteered the information, so I accepted the fact that I didn't have a daddy around. It was just me and her. She had to go through psychiatric treatment and it worked. She took her medication on the regular, but I guess that day the depression won the battle. After that, I didn't even want to walk across the stage. I'd called Yhental before I could even call the police. She, her father, and brother were there in a millisecond to console me. Yhental took me out the house to her dad's car while her brother and father took care of the rest. I don't know what they did, but I knew my mother was cremated and I received a debit card with a whole lotta money on it. At least two mil that I saved for bills and college. I never asked what happened nor did I want to know. I loved my mother, but something about the entire situation that led up to her murder didn't sit right with me. That was four years ago and I still had questions that I didn't have the answers to. There was no one to answer them. They way my mother would act was not of a woman who was raped but one with a broken heart. The hood confirmed it one day when Yhental and I were going to my house. I heard the group of women that always was outside like they didn't have a life, mumbling how my mother was fucking a married man and he chose his family over us. I wanted to punch all those no life bitches in their mouth, but Yhental stopped me. She told me that they were lying but my gut believed them. That was the past and that's exactly where I left it, in the past.

I shook my thoughts as I got dressed and waited for Yhental to pick me up. We were both graduating from Xavier University but I was going to the school of nursing. I still hadn't gotten my acceptance letter but I wasn't tripping because I knew I got in. Yhental said some shit about taking a year off to have some fun before leaving the city, but I wasn't with it at first. Yhental was a real life hermit that didn't go anywhere. A grown ass woman and had yet to see the inside of the club. The only time she did do anything was when our sorors did Greek fest and we went, but she always followed the rules whereas I didn't have any. Her ass was still a virgin but I started fucking at sixteen. I lived my best life, going to clubs and having fun. I would try to get her to come out but her mother always said no. I even ran into her brother a couple of times running through the same clubs and he always looked out for me, buying me drinks and shit.

"What yo' ass daydreaming about? Bring yo' ass, Nay." Yhental walked into my apartment, scaring the shit out of me. I looked her ass up and down and knew she wouldn't have on the romper we agreed on.

"What happened to the romper, bitch?" I asked her as we walked to my front door. I had mine on, wearing it proudly. Whereas Yhental was on the short side, I was an inch or two taller than her. We had the same long hair but mine didn't get curly when it got wet and was thick as hell. I was a shade darker than her and I was all black but I had light brown eyes. I had long legs, thick thighs, and a fat ass. I was a little on the chunky side but I didn't have no love handles or no shit like that because I took gymnastics, so that kept my stomach from getting fat.

"Look, I had to reason with my daddy. In order for me to drive my own car and not have him or BJ bring me, I had to change my outfit after breakfast. He also gave me my black card, bitch, so this shopping trip is on me," she told me, and I laughed. They always did my girl shit like that though. She was a grown woman and still had to go to her parents for permission to do hair, but her mother was the worst. I loved Yhena like she was my mother and she had been nothing but nice to me, but she really needed to chill the fuck out. Like, Big Bakari needed to dick her oriental ass down for her to pipe down and let my girl live.

"Well, I guess it was a win-win because you still look sexy as fuck." I gave her a high five as we walked to her car. That's what I loved about Yhental. She knew I had money but she didn't mind spending hers on me and vice versa. Sometimes when we would sneak to the mall, I would foot the bill and she got whatever she wanted, which wasn't much because she was spoiled as hell. She was the only friend I had and I would have switched lives with her in a heartbeat.

"Do you have gymnastics practice today?" she asked me with a stank face, because I always made her sit through and wait for me to finish.

"No, but we still gotta go to the school and get fitted for our cap and gowns," I told her, and she nodded her head up and down.

After we were fitted for our shit we hit the highway to the Mall of Louisiana. We were getting outfits for one of our soror's birthday party. Of course, we had to wear all red, so I was going to make sure we looked sexy as hell.

"Did you ask your parents to go to the party with me tomorrow night?" I asked her, rolling my eyes. I was going to the party to scope out some new dick to fuck. It had been a minute since I'd had the touch or affection of a man and I needed it desperately. The last nigga I fucked couldn't last long enough for me to get a nut and that pissed me off and I told him to get out. He had been stalking my phone until I blocked him. Then he started calling from different numbers until I blocked every number he called me from. I wasn't changing my number because I'd had it since middle school.

"Bitch, do you know Tyree keep calling my fucking phone from different numbers?" I told her as she hopped off the road and pulled up to the nearest Starbucks. We knew it would be at least an hour and a half before we got to the mall, so we needed something for the road. She ordered us two large mocha velvet crunches and a bottle of water because the shit was too sweet but it tasted so good. She pulled out her card to pay for it and I smiled. My girl was growing up.

"I know he got somebody following me, if not him," she said, handing me my drink. I laughed.

"After all these years, they still have somebody tailing you? That shit crazy," I told her, because it was true. Maybe she knew or didn't know what her family was into, but it was hard for her not to. My girl was green but not that green.

"Yhental, do you know why they were so overprotective over the years and you never get to do shit people our ages do and you never wondered why?" I asked her as she pulled off and we got back on the highway. I loved the way her Camaro glided, and she had a drop top. She let it down once we were on the highway so our hair could blow in the wind.

"I mean, I know what they do for a living is dangerous and

they are just trying to protect me from their enemies, but I know how to protect myself. BJ taught me how to take a gun apart and put it back together, put one in the chamber, and how to aim straight for the dome and empty the clip, so trust me when I say I know how to protect myself," she told me, and I looked at her in awe. I was flabbergasted because this shit was new to me.

"Well damn, when were you going to tell me?" I looked at her.

"When it was your turn." My eyes bucked out my head. I didn't need protection or to learn how to do anything because I wasn't a part of her family and I didn't have no enemies.

"Turn? I don't need a damn turn because I'm not in danger," I told her as she continued to drive.

"Girl please, you been a part of my family since we were kids, and I can't change my father and brother's mind and you can't either, so you stuck with us." She laughed but a smile never graced my face. Just the mention of her brother made my pussy wet.

Bakari Jr, or Mello by the streets, was every bitch wet dream. His creamy mocha skin, long dreads, and light-colored eyes made my heart melt. His body was covered in tattoos that I wanted to run my tongue across. He had to be about 6'4 so he was a giant to my 5'6 frame. When I first met him I was about ten and I was starstruck. Everything about that nigga screamed stranger danger, but I wanted him or at least to taste his damn skin because I knew it would become my favorite flavor. Since a child I craved this nigga. His bow legs made him walk with a slight limp, so I knew his dick hung low and heavy between his legs. I wanted that nigga in the worst way. When I told Yhental about it, she declared her brother off limits, saying that even though she wasn't in the streets she knew he was fucking everything walking and she didn't want Bakari to hurt me. That it would hurt her because I was her best friend. I didn't give a fuck who that nigga was fucking, I wanted a piece too. It wasn't like I was trying to make the nigga my husband, I wanted to sample the dick and mouth.

"I hope that nigga is following us so I can give him a show," I told her as I squatted in my seat and pulled down the top of my romper, shaking my titties.

"Ahhh, Nay, what the fuck are you doing?" She laughed as I sat my ass on the back of the seat and the top half of my romper popped up and down as my titties flew everywhere.

"Mello, if you watching nigga, this show is for you!" I screamed, mashing my breasts together and shaking them with my hands.

"That's it, when we get to the mall, no more drop top for yo' ass," she screamed, and I laughed, falling back in my seat. She should have known I was gon' do some crazy shit because I was a free spirit. If I could walk the earth ass naked I would, because clothes on my body had to be a sin. I laughed until I had tears in my eyes at the look Yhental had on her face.

"I told you that BJ was off limits. I love you too much to share you with my brother. You are my friend and I know my brother," she said, and I cut her off.

"Okay, fuck, I know he a dog ass nigga but I'm trying to be his fucking puppy," I told her, laughing even harder, pissing her off. I knew she didn't even want me speaking to her brother, but I had to tease her. Of course, I wanted to fuck him, but I never would because she was right. He would break my damn heart and the way my mind set up, his hittas would kill me without a second thought and we would be on *Snapped New Orleans*. I valued our friendship far more than dick, even if it was attached to her fine ass brother, so I only teased her when it came to him. I didn't want nothing from him, not even a handshake, because niggas like him really disgusted me. He would fuck any girl he wanted but if a female did it, she was considered a hoe. I guess that's why my friend was still a virgin, and I could almost bet that Yhena only knew what Big B's dick felt like.

"You know I hate when you fantasize about my brother, Nay." She looked at me and rolled her eyes.

"It's all in fun. You know I don't like your brother like that. I had a fucking crush on him since you and I met, but that was when we were ten bitch, but that's water under the bridge." That was all true. Once I found out how he was moving when I got older, my entire fantasy stopped. Now everything was for play.

When I would spend the night at their home for days at a time, I would always steer clear of Bakari. That was until he moved out and I finally started to come out of my shell. I was mad that I missed breakfast this morning, but I was tired and needed the extra sleep.

After driving for about thirty more minutes, we were at the mall. It was packed because school was about to be out, and every age group was out trying to buy the shortest fucking shorts they had to offer. We should have gone to Oakwood Mall, but they didn't have shit. Half the stores were closed or closing, and I knew we wouldn't find shit. She parked the car and pulled the top down, rolling her eyes at me. I laughed because I knew she would be pissed off, but she'd eventually forgive me. I grabbed my keys and purse, and we made our way to the mall for some much-needed shopping

"Which way first?" I asked her, because I knew she wanted to probably go in every fucking store. We had to figure out where or who the fuck was gonna carry all the shit I knew she was going to get. Malls were her favorite outings. She was like a kid in the candy store. She got shit that she needed and didn't need, but I kept my mouth closed because she didn't know when she would be able to come to the mall or anywhere again.

"It don't matter to me. I just came in here to find something red for this party, get something to eat, and get back to the city before the streetlights come on. I don't need the fucking swat team searching for yo' ass," I told her as we walked in the first boutique.

"First of all, my father knows that I'm at the mall but not which mall. He gave me permission to shop until I dropped." She looked at me, and now it was my turn to roll my eyes.

"Bitch, you twenty-one years old. You shouldn't need permission from anyone to go anywhere. You did all the shit they requested from you and yet, you have to ask them to do shit like you 10," I told her and didn't give a fuck if she got mad. Since I'd been knowing Yhental, she always had to ask her parents for permission to do shit. I get that her father was a treacherous man with a lot of enemies so he had to protect them by any means but damn, my girl couldn't even have a life because of the life he lived.

"I don't need you to tell me how old I am because I know when my birthday is. I just got so accustomed to asking them and most of the time my mother says no, so I just don't fucking ask. I went to my father this morning and he told me to have fun." She put her head down. The last thing I wanted was for her to feel bad about her parents' decisions.

"Look, Yhental, I just get mad because for once, do something that you want to do and not have to ask permission from your parents. Make your own decisions because you owe your mother nothing. You are so closed off to life that when they do turn you lose you gon' be dumb to the streets, but that's okay because I got you. Your brother does too. I know it's her that's the hardest because your father wants you happy instead of cooped up in the house. You probably holding on to your virginity because of some sick shit your mother told you when it could actually be a beautiful thing." Yhental knew all about how my virginity was broken and I didn't regret it not one time. Just the nigga that broke it, if that makes sense.

"You're right. I should start to make my own decisions. You know what's funny? I was thinking that same thing this morning. I have done everything that my mother asked of me and that still ain't enough, but BJ can run the streets and even move off the fucking compound. Don't get it twisted, I loved not paying bills and having responsibilities, but I want different. I want to venture out on my own. Why do you think I applied to Spelman for pharmacy school? I wanna get the fuck away from my parents so I can have my own life and do what I want to do. If I stay in New Orleans, the hold will get tighter," she told me as we browsed the racks but couldn't find shit. We left out the store and went to the next.

"Well, you know I'm rolling with you 81/80 with whatever you choose, but I didn't get my acceptance letter yet. I know my grades and shit are good, so what's the hold up?" I questioned more to myself than her. I knew we were taking a year off, but I told her let's just not go the first semester. If I took the whole year off, I may not wanna go. I felt like my bachelor's in medical surgery was enough, but I wanted to do cosmetic surgery, so I had to go to medical school. I wanted to be in the big leagues like Dr. Miami and Dr. Curves.

"And don't forget, we only taking the first semester off. We headed to Hotlanta after the holidays," I reminded her, because I knew she probably forgot.

"I'm glad you said that because I begged them to let me take a year off but now, I know they gon' be happy that I decided to go a little earlier than expected." She smiled, and I smirked because she was still trying to please them. We walked in Macy's and the rep came to us, calling us by our real names because we were known to spend a pretty penny with them.

"How can we help you today Nhairobe and Yhental?" I swear she was the only person that said my name correctly.

"We need red and sexy," I told her as she handed us mimosas.

After an hour of her showing us different shades of red and everything from jumpers to dresses, we'd finally decided what we were going to wear. Yhental picked out a red, halter-top, short romper that barely covered her ass. It was skin tight and the strap around her neck was made of diamonds. I didn't know how she was gonna fit all the ass she had in it, but I knew it was gonna be sexy. I really didn't know how she was gonna get past her mother and father without them noticing. I, on the other hand, had an apple red, two-piece, sequin crop top and short set. I could wear whatever I wanted so y'all know my ass was everywhere. It's funny how me and Yhental were shaped exactly alike but I was taller, so we pretty much shared clothes. After the rep put our outfits in tall bags, we went to the shoe section.

"How you gon' get past the front door with that shit on?" I asked her, and she laughed.

"Girl, the party is on a Friday. Yhena gon' be sleep and my daddy gon' be in his mancave," she told me then moved closer to whisper, "I think my father stepped down from the throne and gave it to BJ because they had a meeting at the house this morning. You know they only conduct business at the compound when shit is serious," she said, and my eyes got big.

"Bitch, I should have gotten up and came to breakfast because I know there was a bunch of fine niggas with big dick energy and long money dangling everywhere." I laughed.

"Ewwww, bitch, them niggas old like my daddy. You just nasty." She gave me the stank face.

"Shidd, then I know they fine. Them niggas was probably in there looking the fucking Sopranos and I missed it because I was sleep." I was mad because just to look at them was a gift.

"I didn't see them. They must've came when I was sleep and left when I was changing my clothes," she told me, and I kissed my lips.

"I always miss the good shit," I pouted and picked up a diamond-encrusted Louboutin heel. "This would be cute with your outfit, and grab one of those diamond clutches for your phone and keys plus your license," I told her, and she took the shoe from me to inspect it.

"I can't wear these shoes, girl. I wanna dance," she told me.

"Girl please, you gon' dance in these heels because they not even that high, and they are not stiletto heels. Nah let's go find me some shoes," I told her as she went to the girl for her size. I was a simple chick. I wanted all eyes to be on my girl because I knew they weren't expecting her to come out. Everybody in the world knew her father and brother but also knew how they were with her. I wanted her to be a big steppa tonight, and she would be. I went to get a simple pair of red bottoms with the red bow on the back and we went to the counter and paid for it.

Of course, she wanted to go to the Apple store. Yhental already had a MacBook pro, iPad pro, iPhone pro max, and air pods. What the hell else could she possible want? I kept my mouth closed as we walked to the store because this was her shopping trip. She went straight to the desktops.

"I need two of these in pink, please," she told the sales rep, and I looked at her funny.

"What the hell you need two for?"

"One of them is for you. It's my gift to you for being my best friend and going through the trenches with me and my parents' rules for so long. Now you got your first college gift. Plus, you was looking so damn sad because you didn't get your letter yet and I know you wanted one, so I'm getting it," she said and left me standing there to go look at the watches. She pointed to the latest watch with the big face.

"You want one too?" she asked me, and I shook my head no because I didn't wear shit like that.

"Well, give me the red one, sir," she told him and scurried away.

"I knew that was you when I saw all that ass standing there." I cringed at the sound of his voice. I once loved the sound of it, especially when he ate my pussy and moaned. I used to crave his dick until he fucked over me. My first love and also my first heartbreak. I hadn't fucked another nigga since him because all of them were all the same. All the chasing and affection was behind one thing, the sea that moved between my thighs. I thought I was in love with him because he was there for me outside of Yhental when my mother died. He kept me together when I felt like I was falling apart, just to fuck a bitch he knew I hated.

"I don't give a fuck who you thought I was, Juju, but bitch, you better keep walking," I told him.

"Bitch, fuck you. You just mad cuz a nigga ain't fucking with you no more, bum ass hoe." I knew he was mad because he had his flunkies with him and I'd disrespected him. He hated that. Juju knew I was far from a bum bitch.

"Right, you did fuck me on numerous occasions, so wouldn't that make you a fucking bum too? Get the fuck outta my face," I told him and pushed him back. One thing about me, I feared no nigga or bitch because they bled just like I did. "And you talking about a bum, but aren't you a worker and not the boss?" I told him, and I knew he was about to smack me but his flunky pulled him back. I noticed Yhental walk behind me in confusion.

"Oh, I see," Juju said, smirking, "You with the boss's princess. Bitch, you ain't nothing but the fucking help," he barked, and I swung on him, punching him in the mouth. They pulled him back as he reached for his mouth and I saw the blood leaking from it. I didn't give a fuck. He should have known not to fucking play with me. I felt a type of way about what he said, even though I knew it wasn't true. Yhental touched my arm to turn me around so she could check my hand, but I yanked away from her.

"I'm good," I told her with attitude that wasn't meant for her.

"Well okay, bitch, I was just checking on your hand for you.". She rolled her eyes before walking back over to the cashier to pay for our stuff. I didn't mean to have an attitude with her, but Juju made me mad with his words. We walked out the store, but she was walking faster than me. I felt like shit because it wasn't her fault. She stopped and turned to me.

"What you wanna eat?" I couldn't even be mad at her attitude, so I kept my cool.

"We could go to Cheesecake Factory," I told her, and we headed to the car. We were packing the computers and other stuff we bought, when we heard a loud noise coming from the left of us. Loud bass was coming from a car, but I knew the song. Our eyes met and we looked to where the music was coming from. She closed the trunk as we watched in awe as they tried to dance. They look like they were having a fucking seizure standing up.

"Bitch, that's our song, you fucking with it?" I looked at her and she smiled. She started walking soon as Meg started rapping

... Bitch, I'm a star, got these niggas wishin'
He say he hungry, this pussy the kitchen
Yeah, that's my dawg, he gon' sit down and listen
Call him a trick and he don't get off—hold up
Bitch, I'm a star, got these niggas wishin'
He say he hungry, this pussy the kitchen
Yeah, that's my dawg, he gon' sit down and listen
Call him a trick and he don't get offended
He know he giving his money to Megan
He know it's very expensive to date me
Told him go put my name on that account
Because when I need money, I ain't tryna, hold up
He know he giving his money to Megan
He know it's very expensive to date me
Told him go put my name on that account
Because when I need money, I ain't tryna wait
... I can't be fucked with, no

We twerked face to face, side by side, left to right, and separately around the girls in the parking lot. I noticed they stopped dancing and figured they must have felt played. I looked at Yhental and winked my eye at her as she bounced her ass like she was bouncing on a dick. I taught my girl that shit. I bent over, making my ass cheeks clap to the beat. Even the niggas started a small crowd and started yelling and pumping us up. We stood up and faced each other then started rapping along with the baby

... You know why these bitches love me? (why?)
'Cause Baby don't give a fuck (what you do?)
I be fixin' the weave while she suckin' my dick
Pull it out, then I titty fuck (uh, uh)
I fuck her from the back and she nasty, killin' her
Know how I give it up (yeah, yeah)
I be cool on 'em, bitch, ain't no pressure (uh-uh)
Till I met this lil' freak, her name Megan (ooh)

This lil' thing here a stallion, look how she walk
Look how she talk, she sexy (muah)
I like when they pretty and ghetto (uh-huh)
Type of bitch that don't even say hello (yeah, yeah)
And whenever we fuck, she be fuckin' me back
Put her in the headlock with my elbow (mmh)
Now she done reversed it
Got up on the dick and ride the shit like a Camaro, uh

We rapped loud as fuck with everybody around us and danced to the beat until I felt someone yanking me from behind by the back of my romper. I looked over at Yhental and she was being dragged by her feet. The music stopped and everybody left us there.

"You really want me to snap y'all fucking neck, huh?!" His voice sent a chill through my veins. How the fuck did he find us, and why was he not gripping his sister's neck instead of mine. I tried to look and see where the fuck Ye was dragged off to, but I couldn't turn my neck.

"Y'all in another fucking city shaking y'all ass like that shit cute. That shit not cute at all, the fuck wrong with y'all? Nigga would think y'all some basic ass bitches and not doctors," he barked in my ear as he said each word. His lips touched my ear and I pushed my ass against him. He must've been too mad to notice because he didn't say shit. I didn't know if I should knuck if you buck or be turned on.

"You act like we were across the fucking country, Mello. We are in Baton Rouge, pipe the fuck down." I was bold as fuck to talk to him like that in front of his right hand.

"I knew yo' fucking mouth was gon' chew off more than you could fucking handle, and that's why I grabbed you first. You talk all that shit but you ain't ready to be piped down, witcho young ass," he whispered the later so Ye couldn't hear him.

"Let my friend go, Bakari. We were just having fun," I heard her yell as Piper held onto her arm. He knew not to grab her like her brother had me, damn near cutting my air supply.

"You don't know them fucking people, Ye. How the fuck dancing in front a bunch of niggas and bitches fun?! They could have kidnapped y'all dumbasses and took y'all shit," he barked at her. It wasn't that serious. We both knew how to defend ourselves, but we really were just having fun.

"Actually, it was a lot of fun, Bakari. I'm a grown ass woman," Ye told him.

"Man, fuck all that. Piper, take Ye with you and I'mma drive her car with dust bucket over here back to the city. Meet me at my condo," he barked out the orders then dragged me to the passenger side of the car. He opened the door and pushed me in. He bent down and reached in the car to grab my seat belt, but I yanked it from him.

"I can put my own fucking seat belt on." I watched his nostrils flare like he wanted to pop me in the mouth, but he knew better. He licked his lips and chuckled as he slammed the door and went to the driver side and hopped in. I chuckled to myself as he mumbled because I knew his insides were on fire.

Bakari (Mello)

I had been tailing them since they left the fucking school. When we stepped in the mall, I lost them. I wasn't really trying to find them because I wanted to get me some shit too. We even noticed the shit that Juju pulled outside the Apple store. I was about to intervene, but I stopped myself just to see how the shit would play out. She handled her business like a lady and that shit was a turn on. I heard the shit the nigga was saying, and she was giving him too much of her energy. It fucked me up to know that nigga popped her cherry though. I ain't think she was having sex. I could tell by the hurt expression on her face that he broke her heart, and she wasn't healed. Maybe she was healed and was mad at herself for fucking with his bum ass. Either way, I wouldn't ask her because it wasn't my business. If he would have put his hands on her I would've killed him in front of everybody. Imagine my surprise when me and Piper walked out the fucking mall and saw a circle around them cheering them on like they were fucking strippers at a twerk fest. I think I even saw niggas throwing money on them as they danced. They did put the bitches out there to shame, because not a bitch from another city or state could dance like the women from New Orleans. I didn't know who I was madder at,

Yhental or Nhairobe. I was glad that my sister felt liberated enough to enjoy herself because Yhena really had a hold on her life. While they were dancing, I really took notice of Nay. She wasn't the little girl who used to work my fucking nerves at the house with Ye. She had grown up and was big healthy. Wide hips, a fat ass, and thick thighs was what I saw in the air. Lil' momma was stacked. I guess I never paid too much attention to her because I looked at her as a little sister, but fuck, she was big Nay now. Ye would kill me if I made a pass at her best friend because she was the sister that Ye never had, and I knew I would hurt her. I shook the thoughts of her ass bouncing up and down as we drove back to the city. The silence in the car was killing me so I connected my phone to the Bluetooth to play some Jeezy. Soon as the music started, Nay reached over and turned the music down. I was about to pop the fuck outta her but had to refrain myself because this was not my car. Then again, it wasn't hers either, but I didn't wanna argue with her.

"Why you got me in the car with you instead of your sister? I wouldn't have minded sitting next to Piper's fine ass," she said, breaking the silence, and I chuckled. I felt the vein popping out my head as I gripped the steering wheel tighter. My foot pressed deeper on the gas, making her head pull back. Her making a reference to my potnah in front of me had a nigga heated, but I didn't know why.

"Aren't you my little sister too? Protect you too, right?" I knew that was a jab to her ego because any nigga with eyes could see that she been crushing on me, but I couldn't do it. I asked her the question so I wouldn't sound jealous. I'd never been a jealous nigga so this was a new feeling.

"We were straight. You could have rode back with Piper and left us alone." She rolled her eyes and that shit was so fucking sexy. Her slanted eyes had me under a spell.

"Watch the fucking road before you kill us!" she yelled at me, and I turned my head back to the road. Nay had just enough hood in her to make a nigga like me go upside her head.

"I'm watching the road. Don't touch the radio," I told her, and she laughed like I said some funny shit.

"You real funny, Mello," she told me through laughs.

"How?" I asked her.

"Nothing, just get me home so I can get away from you." Her hood shit was back, and I was glad. The longer she was silent, and I kept stealing glances at her sexy ass, the more I wanted her in my bed, and that would never happen. I watched as she twisted her body away from me more toward the window, and I shook my head. Little did she know, she wasn't going to the Magnolia project or to the compound. She was coming home with me.

"Where the fuck are you taking me?" Nay finally snapped out her nap and noticed we were in New Orleans Business District and not the slums of the project. That's what I didn't get about Nay. I knew she was sitting on millions, not that I was counting her pockets, but she lived in the project. I didn't know too much about her childhood, but I knew she could be living better than what she was currently.

"I'm about to show you where I lay my head and if I find out you opened yo' mouth, I'll kill you myself." I gave her a hard look and her face turned soft. That was the cutest shit ever. I knew I was making a mistake by bringing her here because her aura was already drawing me in, and I knew she was off limits. I would be good though, because Ye and Piper were gon' be there.

"And not too fucking much on how Piper looks. That shit ain't for you. Plus, he got a girlfriend," I told her to shut any thought she had of fucking with that nigga down.

"I don't give a fuck about his girlfriend because I'm not trying to be her. I'm living my best life, Mello. Niggas cheat all the time, don't you?" Her slanted eyes got low like she had smoked a blunt.

"The fuck can I cheat when I'm single?" I told her honestly.

"Well, I'm sure all the bitches you fucking got boyfriends, but that don't stop you, right?" She cocked her head to the side, twirling her finger my way. I wanted to bite that motherfucker. She oozed sex appeal and didn't even know it. I could smell the vanilla scent that seeped through her pores, and it stirred some shit in me that I ain't never felt before.

"That's their problem. I let them know up front what's up, it's up to them to continue to fuck me. I fuck them and duck them," I told her, and she made a screw face.

"But me and Ye dancing outside isn't ladylike, but yet you are attracted to hoes? Make it make sense," she told me as I pulled into the underground garage to park the car.

"I can't explain the shit. It's like..." I paused and tried to find the words because I wasn't expecting all this motormouth ass conversation. "When a man fucks different bitches, it's cool, but we as men hold certain women to a certain standard," I tried my best to explain, "So to see you and Ye out there dancing like some hood rat bitches had my jaws tight as fuck," I said as I put the car in park.

"So you hold me to a certain standard, huh? And what standard might that be, Mello?" she asked me. Something about the way she said that shit made my dick hard. I hated that she called me by my street name because that meant she only knew the street nigga.

"A standard that yo' ass shouldn't be living in the projects, a fucking standard that a nigga shouldn't be able to get under yo' skin." I paused and realized I fucked up. "I know you had dealings with that nigga Juju, but that shit dead because he the fucking help. Don't associate yoself with niggas like that. I hold you to a standard to know yo' fucking worth and get the fuck out the hood and live a better fucking life. A life that don't involve your life being in danger every fucking day that you open your eyes." I looked at her as I killed the engine. "You deserve better than piss-smelling hallways or niggas trying to grope you every time you pass them going to your apartment. The shit you think I don't see be in a clear eye view, Nhairobe," I told her, exposing my hand. I knew I be on some stalker shit, but she was a part of our family, so it was only right that I looked out for her like I did Ye, but shit with Nay felt different. It was like I loved her like a sister, but she wasn't my sister. I knew moving forward that I had to keep her ass at arm's length. I got out the car and went to the other side to open the door for her. This shit was new to me. I never took the fucking pleasure of opening doors for women. That wasn't my thing. I never even defended a woman the way I did Nay in Baton Rouge. I only fucked bitches and left, but some shit was brewing with Nay's young ass that I couldn't handle. She stepped out the car, pulling her romper down and standing up. She walked away from me to go to the trunk and I couldn't help but watch as her ass cheeks spilled from the bottom. I bit my bottom lip trying to control walking behind her and rubbing my dick through her cheeks.

"What you still standing there for? We got shit to get out the trunk so come on." She snapped me out my thoughts, and I looked at her face.

"Nah, y'all not staying here. I gotta talk to Ye then y'all can go by my parents. You don't need to go back to your apartment tonight because I don't trust that nigga Juju." I knew that nigga knew where she stayed at because that was the only place she ever lived.

"I'm good, Mello, trust me, that nigga ain't that crazy," she told me, but clearly, she didn't understand what the fuck I was saying.

"That wasn't a request, Nay. I'm telling you that you are going to stay with Ye at my parents' house until I say it's safe for you to go home. I'll go over there and get you some shit and bring it to you. You don't know that nigga like I do. He felt played in front his crew so you gotta know he coming for you," I told her, and she stood silent. She walked over to me, getting into my personal space.

"Let me find out you trying to protect what's yours." Her lips were inches from mine with every word she spoke. If I went toward her, I would peck her lips. I had to control grabbing the back of her hair and sticking my tongue down her throat.

"I protect everything that's mine, and that includes you," I told her, walking away, and she followed me to the elevators that led us to my apartment.

When we got to the hallway, I noticed Ye and Piper standing across from each other on different ends of the hallway. Piper walked over to me and handed me my keys.

"Nigga, Ye got a mouth on her when she mad. Next time, she riding with yo' ass." I looked past him at Ye and her eyebrows looked evil. I walked to my door unlocking it and letting the ladies in. Piper had some shit to handle for me so after a few words spoken between us, we dapped up and agreed to meet up later. I needed him to get someone to sit on Juju until I got my money, and he was definitely gon' pay for disrespecting Nay in the mall.

I walked in the door slamming it. I noticed them hugging each other like Celie and Nettie from *The Color Purple*. I wanted to laugh, but I was mad that they were showing their asses in another city. Before I could get a word out, Ye was stomping toward me.

"Why were you following us, Bakari? Daddy said I could do what I want to do," she sassed me, looking like a midget, but I let it slide.

"I'm sure Daddy wouldn't want to know that you were shaking yo' ass in the middle of a fucking parking lot either," I laughed, "Or how about I tell Momma, and you know you would be on lock down for the rest of your life and it would be goodbye to Spelman," I told her, and she folded her arms because she knew I was telling the truth.

"Okaaayyyy, Bakari, it won't happen again. You ain't gotta threaten me." She rolled her eyes and walked away to go to Nay.

"In case Nay didn't tell you, she staying at the house until further notice because I don't trust that nigga Juju since the mall accident, and don't ask how I know, I just do," I answered the question before she could ask.

"You think Mom and Daddy gon' let me go to my line sister's party, BJ?" she asked me.

"Don't worry, you going. I got ya back, just don't make me

regret it, Ye," I told her, and she ran to me and jumped in my arms. I hugged her back and laughed, but my eyes met Nay's. I couldn't decipher what she was thinking or even wanted to say.

"Y'all ride back to the house and I'll stop by Nay's to get the shit that I think she needs and bring it there before I head back out." I kissed Ye's forehead and told Nay, "Bring yo' ass here too, you get a forehead kiss too." I wanted to suck on her lips, but a forehead kiss would do for now.

"See, I told you BJ was a sweet big brother," Ye told me, but Nay's eyes never left mine as they walked out the door. I had to get ahold of the feelings that I felt for Nay because Ye declared her off limits and I had to respect that, right?

Yhental

I was so glad that Nay came to stay with us. I needed the company to keep me away from my mother. She was less and less on my nerves with Nay around, so that was a plus. It was the day of my line sister's party and I was happy as hell to be getting out the house. I had gotten a red trench coat to go over my outfit for the party so that my nosey ass mother didn't see. I just prayed that she was asleep and that my father was in his mancave when we decided to leave. My sis was doing it big for her 25th birthday. Her party was being held at the River City Venues so I knew the aura was going to be elegant with a splash of hood. All the Deltas had to wear red and walk in together, so I was geeked. I'd already taken my shower and sat at my vanity table waiting for Nay to do the same. She pin curled my hair and I put my bonnet on to keep the curl. I lotioned my body with my vanilla Vaseline lotion and only put my red thong on because I didn't need a bra. Nay had gotten me a diamond-encrusted flower to pin to the side of my head. I swear she was always extra when it came to me. Now I was waiting on her slow ass to get out the shower so she could do my makeup. I wanted a light beat with red eye makeup. I already had my lashes done but, of course, I had to have something red on my face. Our nails and feet were done to perfection by the lady that did house calls for my mother.

I was surprised that she was letting me go to the party. I didn't even have to ask. It was either my mother or father that told her to live my life because right after I got out the shower, she called me to her room. I sat on her bed as she began to talk to me.

"Yhental, my sweet baby girl," she said in broken English, but I understood, "I know that I have hard on you your entire life but tonight is about you. I want to go out and enjoy your day like it's your last. Whether it's staying out all night or coming in at a decent hour, just make sure you have fun." Her words cracked, but she continued, "Before I met your father, I was living in hell. My mother and father were barely making it. We lived in the slums of Japan. A hut that housed me, my parents, and my older brother. They always kept close eye on me. All I could do was go to school and come home. I promised myself that if I got the chance to make a better life for myself that I would jump on it." I was surprised that she was telling me this because I never knew how she and my father met. "I left out the house late one night to go down the way to get a drink because we didn't have anything in our hut. I only had a few dollars, and my total came up to more than what I had. I turn to put some of the things back and there was your father, my knight in shining armor. I was dressed in tattered and dirty clothes, my teeth were damn near green, and I didn't have on any shoes. My feet were black and dirty from walking on the sand, but he saw past all that. He saw the beauty that I didn't see in myself. He talked to me, but I didn't understand shit he was saying, but the man behind the counter translated everything that Bakari was saying. At first, I thought he was human trafficker because of the way he was dressed in his cufflinks and expensive clothes, but I later found out he wanted to help me. After that, the rest was history. My family hated him, but I loved him for what he'd done for me. We started out as friends. Him helping me when we got to the states, and we turned to lovers and here we are twenty-five years later with two beautiful kids," she said, and I felt the tears brimming my eyelids. I never knew my mother lived like that before she met my father. "I vowed to myself that I would never raise my kids like my parent raised me and here I am holding you back from being your true self. Baby, I apologize for treating you the way I have been all your life and I ask for your forgiveness," she said, and my stomach churned. I loved the way she expressed herself, but the churning in my stomach made me feel like something bad was about to happen. I tried to shake the feeling, but I couldn't. My mother never sat down with me and told me why she treated me the way she did. I just thought it was her overprotecting me.

"I have something for you. I wanted you to have it when you first turned twenty-one but I felt like you weren't ready, but now I know you are because you are a blossoming young lady," she said and stood from her bed and went to her beautiful dresser to retrieve a box. She pulled out a red rectangular box and walked back over to the bed and sat next to me.

"I always wanted to get you something that would just come from me. I know your father shower you with everything. Things money can and cannot buy, but I wanted get you something that you would look at every day and know that I was the person to give it to you." She handed me the box and I looked down at it. I opened it and it was beautiful ruby red and diamond necklace. My eyes lit up, and she was right. My father had given me a lot of things, but nothing compared to the necklace that was in my hands. Not only was it the first necklace I received but it would forever hold sentimental value because it came from my mother. She only bought me clothes and did her motherly duties, so this was special. She took the necklace out of the case, and I turned around so she could put it on me. She placed it around my neck and clamped it together.

"Now you're perfect. It doesn't matter what happens tonight, just know I love you and always wanted what's best for you, Yhental." I turned to her and kissed her cheek as she did in return. I hugged her and left her to watch TV like she always did. I walked in the hallway and ran into my brother.

"What's up Ye, you 'bout to get ready for the party?" he asked me while smoking a blunt.

"Yeah, and I don't need you to try and ruin my fun," I told him and rolled my eyes.

"If yo' ass dress the right way then I won't ruin yo' damn night," he whispered as I walked past him. I turned around to look at him, and he knew from the look in my eyes that my outfit was out of order.

"I might need you to cover for me. Daddy ain't gon' let me go if he see my outfit and me having a trench coat on gon' give me away. You got somewhere to go?" I asked him, hoping his big ass mouth didn't get too loud.

"You must've bought some shit that has all yo' ass and shit hanging out, or is it too tight?" he asked, and I smiled wide.

"What the fuck you wearing like that, Ye? A fucking sling shot. What the fuck is Nay wearing?" I looked at him weird because he never asked what she was wearing when I did go out with her.

"She wearing something cute too, but why tho'?" I looked at him side eyed because he never asked about Nay. I knew he cared about her like he did me but for the most part, Nay was a grown woman and wore whatever she wanted to wear.

"It's just a fucking question, Ye. Don't you want a favor?" I nodded my head up and down. "Alright then, when I ask yo' ass something then, you answer it," he told me, and I laughed. I knew him better than he thought I did, and he wanted my friend but he knew not to fuck with it. He knew what that would do to me.

"Well, I'll stick around until y'all ready to leave. Text me when y'all, ready." With that he swaggered away from me in the opposite direction. I went back to my room and Nay was just getting out the tub. I sat at my table and waited for her to do her special body routine.

"Bitch, it's 'bout to be some ballers in the room tonight, but wait—" She stopped mid-sentence and looked at my neck. "Oh, you pulling all the diamonds out tonight, huh? Big B ain't sparing no expense tonight? You really showing out," she went on and on before I could even answer her. She was jumping up and down like she just knew I was fucking somebody son tonight.

"First of all, my daddy didn't give me this, Yhena did. She had a whole speech and everything about how she wanted to give this to me my last birthday, but she felt like I wasn't ready, but I was confused because ready for what? I didn't ask her because I was afraid of the answer," I told her and took my makeup out to get started. We were already two hours behind, but we both knew the party would probably last all night. Nay thought she was slick. She wanted to make a grand entrance and I was all for it.

"Yhena know the real. You either 'bout to get that cherry popped tonight or you 'bout to run into your husband tonight. You know Yhena be in her spiritual world. She might've saw some shit coming that we couldn't see or felt some shit that we couldn't feel. Bitch, yo' momma be with the shits. I don't need her telling my future before it happens." I laughed but she was telling the truth. My mother was a very spiritual person. Not like the people that saw spirits and shit, but she felt different energies and knew body language. She knew when people's energy shifted, and she sensed bad energy. If she knew the party would be bad energy for me, I wouldn't be going.

"Nay, come on, we already late and they gon' want us to step," I told her and sat down, pulling my makeup out for her.

"Bitch, with you wearing all those diamonds, Mello and his niggas need not be too far behind," she said, and I raised a brow at her.

"Why the fuck you and him all of a sudden asking about each other? What happened on that ride back from the mall?" I asked her because the shit felt strange.

"What yo' delusional ass talking about? I'm just asking for the added security," she said as she started to apply light foundation because she knew I didn't really like it.

"Bakari caught me in the hallway. I told him that I needed him to cover me because of my outfit and he asked what yo' ass was wearing," I told her, and she looked like she was shocked.

"First of all, yes, Bakari is fine as fuck and I wouldn't mind the nigga dicking me down, but nothing happened in the car and we made a pact, remember?" she said, rolling her eyes. "Bakari is off limits. I know that, so you don't have to make a stank face," she said, and I laughed but she knew. I knew there was an unspoken chemistry there, but I knew they wouldn't do anything because of me.

After 30 minutes of applying makeup that I was probably going to take off before the night was over, she handed me my mirror so I could see her work. I felt sexy and looked even more sexy. My slanted eyes made the diamonds look intensified. The deep shade of red that graced my eyelids was a perfect match to my outfit and matte red lipstick. I smiled because my face was beat for the gods with little to no help.

"I know, I'm the shit. Nah go get dressed while I do something with my face." She pushed me out the chair and sat down.

I went to the bed and pulled my outfit out the bag. I slipped my legs into it and pulled the straps around my neck. I snapped the diamond bracket around my neck. I pulled my bonnet off and took my pins out and watched my hair flow down my back. I grabbed my diamond barrette to put on the left side of my head. My curls fell to my right and down my shoulder.

"Don't forget the Lil' Weezyana Fest is next week before your party, and we going to be good tonight, bitch," she told me, and I laughed. She knew I didn't drink, but tonight I was letting my hair down with my line sisters. I'd suffer the consequences later, tonight was about having fun.

"I'm going to that too. They done fucked up when they let me take this semester off. I'm 'bout to live my best life," I told Nay and kissed her lips, and we both laughed. That was our thing. When we got over excited we kissed. I know it's weird, but we were weird.

I stood up and stepped my freshly red-painted toes into my shoes. By then Nay had done her face and gotten dressed as well and was taking her hair down.

"Biiittcchhhh, you look beautiful. Yeah, you fucking somebody son tonight. I'm glad you waxed and ready," Nay said as I walked to my full-length mirror. I hadn't seen myself yet. I laughed at her antics because I knew I didn't look that fucking good. I stood in the mirror looking at myself. I was giving sex appeal. Hell, I was looking sexy. I couldn't wait to walk the red carpet with her. My face and body were flawless. The red laid perfectly against my skin. I turned to the side and sure as shit stank, my ass cheeks spilled from the bottom of the shorts.

Whap whap

"You better watch all that ass clapping behind you." Nay smacked my ass cheeks as she walked past me, and I laughed. I looked at her and she looked so cute.

"Oh, it's giving," I told her, and it was. Her outfit fit all the right places like a glove and left little to the imagination.

"Oh, you gotta know I'm fucking somebody daddy, brother, son, or uncle tonight. Ain't shit shy about me. You the one that clam up when a nigga look at you too hard," she laughed.

"Not once that brown get in me," I told her, and she knew it was true. Once I got to drinking, all bets were off.

"Let's go before we be too late to the party," she told me, and I picked up my phone to text BJ. A few minutes later I opened my room door and there he was, standing with his eyes glued to his phone. I grabbed my trench coat and threw it over my body.

"We ready," I told him, and he turned around to take us both in. He pulled the lapel of my coat and looked behind me at Nay.

"Oh, fuck no! Y'all ain't wearing that shit to no party, go change now!" he barked at us like we were kids. I heard Nay let out a hard sigh, and I put my head down.

"Nah, fuck that, don't put your head down. Bitch, we spent hours to look like this and this is how the fuck we leaving out this bitch. We don't need Mello to escort us out of here. We 'bout to be lit with or without him." Nay had attitude, and I knew BJ was about to go off.

"Y'all like testing a nigga's patience I see, but y'all can have that because I ain't blocking a fucking view for y'all and Big B is in the living room." He laughed before licking his lips at Nay. I wanted to cry because I knew he was being petty, but I was a grown woman and was not changing my clothes.

"Nobody don't care Mello, we walking out that door just as we are, and you can tail behind us all you want, but my girl having fun tonight." Nay came from behind me and got into his space. That nigga stood silent. All the shit he talked on the regular, Nay had shut his ass down. He backed up, looking her up and down as she walked past him. He licked his lips and ran his hand through his dreads and looked at me.

"Ya girl gon' get herself fucked up playing with me like that."

"Boy bye, either you rolling or you folding," I told him and threw my trench coat back on the bed and walked past him with my clutch in hand. I didn't care what either of them had to say when we walked out the door.

Khaza

"Nigga, it's too fucking late to beg for your life now. You 'bout to die, nigga," I barked at whoever he was through my mask. My brothers thought I was crazy but to me, killing was better than getting the best head and pussy from the baddest bitch. I would rather torture a nigga than fuck, so maybe something was wrong with me.

"Yo' fucking mother is evil just like you. I know she had something to do with this shit. I know she sent the craziest of her fucking sons. Nigga, you ain't gotta hide ya face," he barked as blood mixed with spit flew from his mouth. He was right, but I wouldn't acknowledge it.

Khaya, my mother, was as evil as they came, and I didn't know why. I also didn't know why the fuck she had me torturing her husband, who was also our father. I couldn't tell her no because she was me and I was her, if that made sense. If the shoe was on the other foot, Khaya wouldn't hesitate to empty a clip on a bitch that played with me. I don't know what my father did to have him in this fucked-up situation, but I didn't give a fuck either. I was as heartless as they came when it came to my mother. She was my everything and her word was law. If she wanted me to air out the entire world, I would die trying.

"I don't know what you speak of, sir, but I can assure you that you don't know my mother." I laughed as I looked at him. I had him in the basement of my warehouse on my surgery table ass naked. I had taken the liberty to chain his arms and legs down so he couldn't squirm like a fish. I had a sock in his mouth but took it out because I wanted to hear his last words. That's what I loved the most, making niggas beg for their lives.

"I didn't do that scandalous bitch nothing. I gave her 27 years of my fucking life. I gave that bitch the game and now she trying to take over. She wanna eliminate me so she and our fucking kids can take over the empire I built." He kept talking and I yawned, tired of hearing his bullshit. I had already cut his fingers and toes off and put them in a sterile container to bring back to my mother as proof. I thought the two days I left his ass down here that he would have been dead by now, but clearly this nigga was bad grass that refused to die. My phone vibrating made me tune out his words. I removed my black glove and pulled my phone from my pocket. I looked at the screen at it was Khazeem, my oldest brother.

"What nigga, I'm busy," I answered, because he knew what the fuck I was doing. He knew I hated to be interrupted when I was doing my job.

"Nigga, you ain't finished yet? The fuck she got you doing to this nigga like that?" he asked, laughing. "Or did you come up with your own remedy of torture for this nigga?" He laughed, knowing that if Khaya asked his scary ass to kill somebody, he wouldn't bust a fucking grape in a fruit fight.

Of course, my mother and father ran the Montiago Mafia. They did everything together. Made shipments of heroine, guns, and fentanyl and make sure it got where it needed to be. At one point my mother would be in the chop shop. That's the warehouse where the drugs went. She would be down there breaking down the product to make sure people didn't fuck up. Khay, my father, taught her everything to say and not to say when it came to the drug business. That was until Khaya found some bitches she ran with in Atlanta and gave them a job. They were either hungry college students or hood chicks looking for an easy come up. They were required to be ass naked in nothing but an apron in the room as they measured, cooked, and bagged the product and prepared it for shipment up north. The guns stayed close to home. I owned a warehouse in Alpharetta close to my house so I could sort out the weapons myself. We got everything from rifles to knives shipped from Cuba on a monthly basis. I personally drove the 18-wheeler to my warehouse to disperse the weapons. Khazeem was in charge of the money, making sure it was accounted for.

Khaya made sure everything was up to par, and everything ran smoothly because of Khay. I don't know what this nigga did this time to cause her to kill him, but it had to be detrimental. A while back she caught him fucking one of the college girls in the dope house and cut his thumb off. This nigga was walking round like a sick puppy with no fucking thumb for weeks. I'd asked my mother what happened and she said she cut his thumb off because he probably had his thumb in the bitch ass he was fucking. I laughed the entire night behind that, so I could imagine why she ordered the hit on his ass.

"Nigga, the jet pulling out in two hours, and tell that nigga shut the fuck up," Khazeem said loud as fuck in my ear. "Are you even packed, nigga?" he barked on the phone like I was his fucking child.

"If you must continue to stop me from doing my fucking job, I had a la bitch I fuck with pack my shit and bring it to Mom's, and she put it on the fucking jet! Nah let me finish fucking this nigga up." An evil grin graced my face under the mask as I disconnected the call. I didn't feel like hearing his fucking mouth about me being late. I still had to kill this nigga and bring this shit to my mother before I even boarded the jet. I wasn't tripping because my momma would move the fucking earth for me, so if they had to wait then they would.

I was always a killer though. My father's men trained me and my brothers in every way possible. I could kill a nigga with my bare hands, but I preferred torture. I graduated with my bachelor's in psychology because Khaya wasn't going for that work for the family and me shit. She always told each of us that if this gang and drug shit ever had to end, we needed something to fall back on. College was fun, but I was glad when I graduated. I was officially a Kappa man. I only did the shit because outside of the college parties, pledging was the only thrill I had when inflicting and receiving pain. That's how I got the line name Kellz. One of my big line brothers said I was the pied piper because all the young girls wanted me, and I looked old enough to be their uncle. Standing at 6'3, my muscular physique was giving the Incredible Hulk. I kept my waves on swim and my beard and goatee on trim. That matched with my swag and light brown eyes, the niggas hated me, but bitches loved me. Then my brothers came down the line because we were all a year apart, but them niggas pledged different fraternities. They could fill y'all in on that because I had some shit to handle.

"Kill me, nigga! I know the monster you have become. The monster that Khaya created within you, but it's just you though. You ever think about why she did that shit?" he asked me as life slowly left his body. I didn't give a fuck if he knew who the fuck I was because he was gonna die anyway. His words were fucking with me, but I wouldn't give him the benefit of seeing it on my face. I often wondered why she made me the killer versus my brothers, but I just chunked it up as something she saw in me that she didn't see in my brothers. It wasn't like she was forcing me to do it. I loved the shit. His words were getting at me, and it was time for his lights to go out. I grabbed my scapula and neared him. I pierced the layer of skin right above his heart and cut until he bled. He'd passed out before I could get to the third layer, so it was silent. I carved his heart out his chest and held it as it dripped blood down my hand and sleeve. I stared at his heart as it pumped before putting it on ice and closed the cooler. I grabbed his fingers and toes and put them in a bag. I called my cleanup crew while I undressed and grabbed my shit and headed to my mother's house.

I walked in my mother's mansion, and she was sitting at the head of the table with my brothers around her. I walked straight to her and dropped the bag and cooler on the table. She tilted her head back and winked her eye at me and did a head nod for me to take my seat. I noticed the smug loon on Khazeem and Khamakazee's faces because they hated what I did for the family business. My mother clapped her hands three times, and three men walked in wearing all black. They took the cooler that held the heart and left just as quickly as they came in.

"That heart is going to Cuba, and tell Juan I said thanks." One man turned around and tilted his hat before walking away.

"Ma, what the fuck was that all about?" Khazeem asked my mother, and she smiled at him.

My mother was a beautiful black woman. She had blue eyes with chocolate blended with mocha skin. She was short as hell, about 5'3, and we towered over her. She was beautiful but deadly, and that's what hooked a nigga every time. That's what hooked my father and ultimately became his demise.

"I know you not questioning me in my fucking house but to answer your question, the nigga had to go because I said so, and if you got a problem with that yo' demise can be given too, nigga." She got out her seat and I stood as well. The last thing I wanted was those two to get into it because that shit was never ending. We would never get on the flight to New Orleans.

"Look, cut all that fussing out. The nigga needed to be dealt with and it's handled. Let's talk about this trip to New Orleans." I looked at all of them because I knew if the fussing continued, I would get a headache. I couldn't take the loud noise and shit, so it's best if we get the fuck and soon.

"You act like she the Queen of fucking England or some shit, like a nigga can't ask questions. That was our father that you just killed, and yet you have no remorse for it." Khazeem looked at me with fire in his eyes. I knew he loved our father but if he had to die, I knew it was for good reason.

"I don't have remorse for nothing I do, so what would change now, nigga, the fuck?!" I was toe to toe with Khazeem. I would never fight my brother, but he was pushing it.

"Listen, I had your father killed for reasons that I will not explain because I don't have to. Y'all are my fucking children and if I move a little different, that's my choice. Your father did some shit that y'all wouldn't understand, so I dealt with shit the way I wanted to, and don't question me, Khazeem." She looked at him and he put his head down.

"Hold yo' head up, Khazeem." Her face softened as she looked at him. She always babied him. I'm guessing because he was the middle child and required a little more attention. She left her seat and went to him, giving him a hug and whispering probably some bullshit in his ear, and he smiled. She had all of us under different spells because she never spoke sweet to me, hugs yeah, but anything else affectionate was out of the question. She always said that I looked mean as fuck and we both laughed it off. Truth was that I wasn't a soft nigga. A simple slap on the back or a knot of money would suffice in place of the affection. I knew my mother loved me, but she told me as a child that I never liked affection so that's what I went with.

"Ya cousin Muni is having a birthday party and y'all know she pledged Delta a few years back. I know all y'all in some type of fraternity shit. That's the perfect opportunity to blend in. It's in the heart of New Orleans and y'all need to leave now," she told us, and we stood to our feet. One by one, we went to her and kissed her cheek then her hands before leaving the room. I headed in a different direction from them niggas. They probably had to go home and pack, but I was about to head to the jet and smoke a blunt until they decided to show up.

Khazeem

"You gotta get the fuck out of here," I barked as I walked through my house and into my bedroom. Fucking with my brothers in Magic City last night, I brought a stripper bitch from the club home with me last night. Well, one of my many homes, but this was the one I used when I wanted to bring some pussy home. I watched her stir in her sleep like the fuck she didn't hear me. I pulled the cover from her body slowly and I can't lie, the bitch was bad, but I didn't even remember her name. She had to go. She was a chocolate drop with a build-a-body ass and titties and the flattest stomach that only a surgeon could provide. She couldn't even take the dick in her mouth or her pussy, so why the fuck was she tired. I shook my head as I looked at her sleep so peacefully, but I was about to ruin it.

"Man, get the fuck up, you gotta go." I grabbed her ankles, sliding her to the end of the bed. She tried to kick but quickly realized that I held her ankles hostage.

"What the fuck is wrong with you, Khazeem?! You brought me here!" she screamed, half asleep, giving me a fucking headache.

"And now I'm putting you the fuck out," I told her calmly because I had shit to do, and I felt like she was about to show her ass and I wasn't with it. I let her ankles go and she stood to her feet to scramble to pick up her clothes that were scattered around the house. I watched as she put her clothes on and went into my pocket to get a knot of money. I didn't even know how much was in the roll and didn't give a fuck. As she walked past me, I grabbed her arm to stop her steps. I dropped the money in her hand, and she looked at it before looking at me with disgust.

"Fuck you, Khazeem," she said but didn't attempt to give me the money back.

"Exactly bitch, that's why I gave you this money," I told her as she walked out my room and out the door.

I didn't give a fuck about what she was saying because I had to keep it moving. I grabbed my suitcases and other shit I wanted to bring on this stay we were having in New Orleans, because it definitely wasn't about to be our new home. I didn't give a fuck what my mother said, it was just a vacation.

I was the middle child with Khazeem being the oldest and Khamakazee, or Khay for short, was the youngest. He hated that nickname because he hated our father, but we called him that anyway. Whereas my brothers were chocolate, I was the vanilla one with freckles scattered all over my body and I hated it. My eyes were green and looked transparent according to my mother. I looked more like my father than them. I was the complete opposite of my entire family. I wasn't trained to kill or defend myself like Khaza was, but I knew how to protect my heart.

I was the accountant in the family. Any money that went out and came in had to come through me. I had my bachelor's in business admin with a minor in accounting but pushed more toward accounting. I didn't touch the illegal shit unless it was money. I was a lover not a fighter. I wanted and needed the affection of a woman. Maybe that's why I brought a female home with me every time we went to the strip club. Coming up as a young boy, my mother always showered me with her hugs and kisses. She damn near smothered me in my teenage years. I went to college to escape her and clung to my brother. Then I started to suffer from separation anxiety and pledged Omega Psi Phi. I noticed when I stepped on campus that all the women loved me. I needed that comfort because my mother was back at home with my father. Fucking different females and even just lying next to many was comforting to me. That and being a part of a brotherhood so strong and valuable got me through it. I snapped out my trek down college lane and continued to pack my shit for this trip to New Orleans. I hopped in my car and headed to the strip to meet my brothers because I knew I would be the last to show up. The attendant took my luggage and I walked on the plane and clouds of smoke surrounded me. I could hear their laughing before I could actually see them.

"Man, sit yo' nervous ass down. Khaya only a flight away. This nigga got separation anxiety for real. Sit down and hit the blunt, nigga," Khaza said, and I sat next to him and took the blunt from him, but he wasn't lying. My mother was mean as hell, even vicious, but she was my sweetheart. I pulled out my phone about to dial her number, but Khay stopped me.

"Man, she know we on the plane, put that fucking phone up and enjoy the ride, ole baby ass nigga," he said, and they laughed at my expense. I put my head down and slid my phone back in my pocket.

"I was just calling to check on her. She by herself now." I looked at Khaza with sad eyes.

"Nigga, she got men around 24/7 and Daddy being dead has been swept under the rug. She straight," Khay said, shaking his head, "This nigga a momma's boy for real," Khaza said as I inhaled the blunt. I let the smoke in through my mouth and out my nose and let the weed take effect. I was gonna need this high because I didn't know what I was walking into when we landed.

After getting everything settled in our separate homes in Eastover, we all met up at Khaza's crib. Since it was Muni, I knew she would probably have on her Delta colors, so I had my purple V-neck polo with the yellow horse with my skinny jeans and Jordans to match. My light brown dreads were freshly twisted and crinkled. I was on a prowl tonight because I knew all the sororities and fraternities were gonna be out tonight. Niggas I ain't talk to since college were gon' be there. I looked at my brothers and they wore their colors as well. Khaya really hooked us up but didn't make shit too flashy. She ordered us each a Porsche with personalized plates, but tonight we were riding in the G Wagon. That was labeled our family car. We hopped in and headed to the party.

After twenty minutes of driving, we pulled up to River City Venues. The line was long as hell, but this was Muni we were talking about. She was popular in almost every state, and deadly. Like most of us, we all had a mask that fell off, and Muni was just as deadly as my mother but more silent with her approach. Her hands were lethal, but she had the book smarts like us. She didn't have many friends but moved to New Orleans to get away from the drug life. The irony of her becoming a pharmacist. It was in her blood.

"Man, you see the bitches out here tonight?" That was Khaza with his eyes wide as his fucking face. I looked but didn't see anything eye catching, but they were still outside. We parked in front the club and the valet guy came for the keys. There was a red carpet that rolled before us and we stepped out. Our brothers were stomping in line and our sisters were screaming shit that I didn't understand. We held our signs up, saluting our brothers as we bypassed the line to gain entrance. The party was in full swing, and I was ready to get my drink on. We had already faced two blunts on the way, so I needed a drink to maintain the feeling I felt. I couldn't drink too much because I had to watch Khaza's ass because we were in a new city where we didn't know anyone, and this nigga was crazy, crazy. We went to the bar and got shots of henny to kick the night off. I looked at Khaza as he downed his second shot.

"Nigga, I don't need you watching me. I'mma grown ass man and know how to stay outta trouble. I don't know half the niggas here and ain't trying to start no shit," he said, and I gave him the side eye because I knew better. If a nigga or bitch so much as brushed his shoulder or stepped on his foot by accident, he would pop off and we would have to deal with the aftermath because there was no turning off with his ass. The DJ was playing some hot shit as I bopped my head to the beat. We walked through the crowd and they parted like they knew who the fuck we were. Niggas were mugging and the bitches were salivating at the mouth. With Khaza in front of me and Khay in the back, I walked through until we found a table to sit at and peep the scene. Everything was red including the ice sculpture of the Delta emblem that was spray painted red. The tables were decorated with red and tan cloths with some type of confetti shit on it. The vibe was chill, but I knew it would be a matter of time before they started stepping. I noticed Muni and a female laughing and joking like they were long-lost friends. The female's smile was contagious, and I couldn't help but to smile. She had on all red which meant she was a Delta. The diamond symbol placed on the side of her face couldn't be missed. She was beautiful. Her chocolate skin glistened under the dim light and her eyes sparkled at whatever Muni was telling her. They smiled as they took shots, but I couldn't take my eyes off her as we sat in our section. I felt the shots take effect as I watched the beauty from afar. By the end of the night, I was going to have her or at least talk to her.

"This nigga found him a Khaya," Khay said above the music, and Khaza laughed.

"You laughing now, nigga, but they probably got somebody here to thaw that ice you got around yo' heart and turn it to water," I told him, and he instantly stopped laughing.

"The day that shit happens, I'll walk on water, nigga," he said as we sat back and enjoyed the view.

I couldn't take my eyes away from lil' momma as she hugged Muni and walked away from the bar with two shots. I had a second thought that she was bringing that shit to her nigga, but that wouldn't stop me from approaching because I was confident in what I brought to the table.

"Stop staring and go get her," Khaza said. I noticed Muni

coming toward our table smiling. We stood as she approached, each of us giving her a hug and kiss on the cheek.

"Y'all finally made it!" She jumped with glee. "But why are you sitting down here with everyone else? I have a VIP room set up for you guys, come on," she said, and we got up to follow her.

We ended up on the second floor of the club in a section cut off from the entire party. Red ropes closed off where we were sitting and there were bottles of different liquor everywhere. Pre-rolled blunts sat in the container, and Khaza was the first to speak.

"Man, I'm not smoking some shit I didn't roll myself," he said, and we all laughed. Khaza never smoked a blunt that he couldn't roll himself or see the weed that was put in it.

"I know you don't, that's why I got your stash behind the counter at the bar." She pointed down to the bar where there was a girl looking at us, and she winked her eye. "My girl at the bar got you," Muni said and walked out before letting us know that she would send waitresses up with food for us to eat. As she walked down the stairs, the DJ stopped the music. Everybody downstairs parted like an angel of God had entered the room. I saw Muni rush further down the stairs. I got up to walk to the railing and watched as the Deltas stepped in, twirling their heads. They all had heels on, but the one I had my eyes on was the second woman in line. I felt Khaza get up to join me at the balcony.

"Man, who the fuck is that?" I heard him say under his breath. I followed his eyes to the first girl leading the pack. She was fine but not like the chocolate drop that I'd laid my eyes in earlier.

KHAZA

I had to be fucking dreaming. My heart palpitated like I was having a wet dream. I felt my nuts tightened. Muscles flex. I needed another shot or another blunt because my mind was not my own. She was fucking gorgeous. I noticed her when I first walked in, but I noticed everything. I bypassed the way I felt when I first laid eyes on her because I was ready to have some fun with my brothers. A woman never caught my eyes like the one before me. The way her ass spilled from under the jumpsuit or whatever it was she had on had me in a daze. Some shit higher than weed could take me. She was dripping in diamonds, so I knew she had money, not that I cared. I watched as she stomped with heels on and led her sisters to formation to Silk Sonic's "Leave the Door Open."

What you doing? (What you doing?)
Where you at? (Where you at?)
Oh, you got plans? (You got plans?)
Don't say that (shut your trap)
I'm sipping wine (sip, sip) in a robe (drip, drip)
I look too good (look too good) to be alone (woo-woo)

My house clean (house clean), my pool warm (pool warm)
Just shaved (smooth like a newborn)
We should be dancing, romancing
In the east wing and the west wing
Of this mansion, what's happening?

They stumped to the beat of the song as I watched in awe. I could tell she was short and thick as fuck by the way she moved so effortlessly. Her body moved to the beat like it came naturally. Her body rolled as her leg was held high in the air, and I wondered what they would feel like wrapped around my waist. Her hands made the diamond symbol as she stuck her tongue out and looked at her sisters. The way her tongue rolled across her teeth made my dick jump. I didn't know who the fuck she was, but I was definitely about to find out. She had diamonds all over her body including her eyelids, and I wanted her. Everything about her turned me on. Her thick thighs, chunky waistline, and beautiful face had me drawn to her. I'd never been drawn to any woman, but she had a nigga ready to walk down there and yank her ass out the line. If I could see her ass hanging out from her outfit, I knew other niggas could and I didn't like that. I took a deep breath and continued to watch as her hands went in the air and her hips and ass twerked from left to right. Her diamonds were damn near blinding me so I had to know who she was. I bopped my head to the music and they squatted down as the next verse played.

Ooh, you're so sweet (so sweet), so tight (so tight)
I won't bite (ah-ah), unless you like (unless you like)
If you smoke (what you smoke?) I got the haze (Purple Haze)
And if you're hungry, girl, I got fillets (woo-woo)
Ooh, baby, don't keep me (waiting)
There's so much love we could be making (shamone)
I'm talking kissing, cuddling

Rose petals in the bathtub
Girl, let's jump in, it's bubbling

I watched as the entire line squatted with their hands in the air and rolled their hips in a circular motion to the beat. Ole girl was being extra. She was smiling with her tongue out, enticing the crowd, and they went wild. Niggas were whistling as she bounced her ass in a circle with her line. They slapped the floor and came up rolling their hips in the same motion until the song went off. Then I noticed her stand up and slap hands with Muni and the chick Khazeem had been eye fucking since we got here. That's a one up I had because she was cool with my cousin. I walked toward the stairs, never taking my eyes off her as she went to the bar and ordered two shots. She downed the first one and walked away with the second one. I finished the rest of my blunt as I made my way through the crowd. My eyes never left her body as a slow song dropped. She was winding her hips with her hands in the air, shot in the left. The closer I got to her the shorter she got. She had to be at least 5'2. She swung her hair to one side and popped her hips. I was about four feet from her when a nigga from my fraternity approached her and started to dance behind her. I stood back and watched to gauge her reaction, but she must've been faded because she didn't stop his hand from grabbing her waist and pulling her against him. That shit made my blood boil through my veins, and I didn't even know her. Something about her face held an innocence that I felt the need to protect. Even through the makeup and her being cross faded, I knew this wasn't her scene. When she realized that the nigga was kissing in her neck, I noticed her body tensed. She quickly tried to remove his hand, but he was adamant on holding her tight. Her neck twirled like she was arguing with him as she turned to face him. The party kept moving like normal, but I tuned that shit out and had tunnel vision on her. I hadn't realized that my feet were moving until the nigga grabbed her neck and I had my gun to the back of his head.

"Nigga, let her go." I put one in the chamber, and he tried to move but the hold I had on the back of his neck caused him to remain still. His hands went up in surrender, and she backed away from him and slapped his face.

"The fuck is wrong with you, nigga. Do you know who my father and brother are? They will fucking kill you!" she yelled in his face before hitting him again. That piqued my interest. Who the fuck was her brother and father, and why should anyone fear them? I kept that in my mental for a later date to discuss with my brothers.

"Do you have a fucking problem with yo' hands, nigga? If you do, I can solve it." I pushed the gun further into the back of his head.

"Khaza?" I heard him say my name and I let him go. He turned my way and I noticed it was one of my line brothers when I pledged.

"Nigga, I was about to smoke yo' ass," I told him, tucking my gun away.

"That's you, nigga?" he asked as ole girl walked away from us and to Muni and some other chick. I didn't know how to answer him because I didn't even know who the fuck she was.

"Nah nigga, you just need to keep your hands to yourself," I told him and walked away back to my brothers.

"Nigga, how the fuck did you get that past the metal detectors?" Khay asked once I met them at the bottom of the steps.

"I went around them, the fuck you mean? I can't travel without at least one gun," I told them, and they laughed. I did a brief survey around the club looking for her and found her by the table standing with her girls and a nigga that was rubbing her cheek in a loving way. I walked in their direction with my brothers not too far because they knew how I could get when provoked, and we didn't want no beef our first night in New Orleans.

"This him right here," I heard her angelic voice above the bass say to the dude that towered over her. He turned to me and my brothers.

"Aye, thanks for protecting my sister. I owe you," he chuckled and continued, "But if it was my gun, that nigga would be kicking dirt." He continued to laugh, and I joined in.

"That shit not funny, Mello! You always wanna spoil the fucking fun," lil' bit screamed and walked in front her brother and was now in my space. I could smell her vanilla scent mixed with whatever she was drinking. Her blue eyes were low like she'd been smoking, but she didn't strike me as the type.

"Thanks...." she said, dragging the word out because she didn't know my name.

"Kellz," I offered her because I wasn't about to give her my real name. I gave her a head nod.

"Ye," she said, and I knew that wasn't her real name, but I'd take that for now. She walked off with her friends and brother, and a wicked grin graced my face.

"This nigga about to stalk this girl all night until he get her alone," Khazeem said and laughed because it was the truth. They both knew how obsessive I could become once I had my thoughts fixated on something. I walked away from them and went to the bar to order a shot because I wasn't about to walk back to our section without getting her number. I could have gone to Muni and talked her into getting it, but I wanted to do shit my way. Plus, I wanted to figure who the fuck her brother was, and what better way to find out? I took my seat on the stool and smoked my blunt. I ordered two shots and downed them as I scanned the crowd looking for her. My brothers had separated but I knew they weren't too far.

I got tunnel vision when I heard a little chatter from my far left. It was her and her friends. Some slow shit was playing, and they were pushing her to the middle of the dance floor, but she was shy. The more they pushed her, the more she pushed back until they were in the middle of the dancefloor. The song must've been her favorite because I could see her face flush through the dim club. The slow rhythmic song moved through her body and took over. With her head down she started to move her hips as her hands made circles in the air. Her thighs parted as she dropped down in a slow wind, and everybody moved out of her way. She controlled the dancefloor. There were others dancing around her but everybody's attention was on her. Her body came up like a snake and she did some pop shit, and I knew I had to make my move. I hadn't realized my feet were moving until I was within a few feet of her. By then she was on her feet, rocking her hips from left to right in slow motion. I looked at Muni and she winked at me, but a smile didn't quite make her face, and I didn't know what that was all about, but I'd find out later. I walked up on her, towering over her short ass, and started moving against her. All the dancing she did, I could still smell the hint of vanilla on her skin. She moved against me as I wrapped my arm around her waist as we moved in sync with each other. My imagination was running wild from the way she twirled her hips against me. I thought how she would ride my dick and fucking her doggystyle. She dipped in front of me with her hands in the air, sliding down the bottom half of my body. She had my head gone. I was about to nut in pants, and I didn't even know her. I could make her body tremble if she was fucking with it. She came back up, teasing a nigga, and rocked against me. I bent a little so she could feel how hard she had my dick and whispered in her ear.

"Let me make ya legs shake." I heard a slight moan and her arm reached up to wrap around my neck. I could hear Muni and the other girl cheering her on as she danced harder against me. I held her tighter, trying to stop her movements, but I couldn't. She was in control. I swiftly turned her around to face me and I could tell she was cross faded. She had been drinking and smoking. Her eyes were low as she smiled, trying to put her arms around my neck. I put my mouth in the crook of her neck and kissed there. She tensed. All the grinding she was doing on a nigga, but now that she'd faced me, she wanted to freeze up. Nah, I needed the same energy she had when her back as to me. She looked up at me and started to back away, but I held her in the moment with me.

"Nooo," she dragged out and tried to get away with little resistance. If she really wanted me to let her go, she could have gotten away. Something in her eyes was playing tug a war and I couldn't figure it out. It was like she wanted to stay but something was moving her feet away. I pulled her closer to me with a little force.

"I know you feel that shit." I pressed her top to mine so she could feel how hard my heart was beating. This was some spiritual shit that I was on. I wanted her in more than one way.

"I can't do this. I don't even know you, and my brother is—" My finger to her lips stopped her words. I didn't give a fuck about who or what her brother was. I wanted her to stay in this moment with me. We could think about tomorrow when it came but for right now, I wanted her.

"Man, fuck yo' brother and whoever he is. Do you know who the fuck my brothers are? Better yet, do you know who the fuck I am?" I reversed the question, and she looked at me with slanted eyes. Her eyes held a scared yet innocent look that I couldn't put my finger on. They were almost hypnotizing. I gave her a mug and she piped down. If only she knew who or where the fuck I came from and who my mother was, she wouldn't even mention her brother or anyone else in her family. "Whoever the nigga is, he don't put fear in me." I had to remember I didn't know her or her family to be judging. I was outside my body already and didn't even know what the pussy tasted like, but I was drawn to her and tonight I would figure out why. She was like a witch I was hunting or a puzzle I was trying to figure out. If she had me this curious on sight, I could only imagine about the magic between her legs. I wanted to know her. It was like a craving for my favorite food. The best strain of weed I'd ever smoked and still wanted more. Chasing my very first high but couldn't quite reach it. I wanted to know her inside and out. I hadn't realized that we stopped dancing until Muni tugged at my arm, pulling us apart.

"That ain't the move, cousin," she tried to whisper in my ear but by then, my brothers had walked up and heard everything.

"What the fuck is so special about her people that I can't fuck with her? These niggas God or something?" I yanked my arm out her grasp and she smiled. Muni knew the monster I could become.

"Nah, it ain't that. They just protective over her, like follow her around protective. She's the only girl and her brother is dangerous," she said lowly.

"The fuck you mean dangerous?! That nigga bleed just like I bleed. If I want his fucking sister then I'll have her. The fuck outta my face with that dumb shit like you don't know how I'm coming," I told her then thought about it, because pussy wasn't worth beefing with no nigga. "But you right, I don't know her or her people but I wanna get to know her, and who gon' fucking stop me? She the only one that could and even if she do, she can't because you know how persistent I get when I want something." I looked at Ye to see her facial expression, which held none.

"First of all, I am not a piece of cloth that you own. I am a woman. If you wanna get to know me then I'm with it, and you're right, I do wanna get to know you," she whispered in my face, and I smiled. I see she liked a nigga to be rough with her. It was in her eyes. "Look, y'all killed my buzz or whatever I had going on. Am I leaving with you or not?" she asked me, smiling, and reached for my hand. I didn't trust that wicked smile, but I knew I could handle it. She had something up her sleeve and I was curious to find out. I looked back at Muni, her friend, and my brothers before grabbing her hand in mine and sticking my tongue out. Clearly, she didn't give a fuck about who her people was, so I was going with the flow of shit and crossing that bridge when we got to it, if it ever came.

Nhairobe

I was a wild bitch, but I knew Ye wasn't. She was pulling moves that I pulled when I went to the club. This wasn't her. I hoped she didn't take what I said back when we were getting dressed as some type of dare shit, because that's not what it was. Bringing niggas home or going to their place after the club was my thing. In her case, she had to be going to wherever he lived because Big B would kill that nigga at the gate.

After they left, the party was back in full swing. I made sure to turn on my location and to track Ye because she was on my dime and I didn't want to hear Mello's mouth. I wanted my girl to let loose at least once in her life. I felt she was safe with Khaza, even though he looked mean as fuck. I knew he wouldn't hurt her. His vibe was different. He and the niggas he was rolling with stuck out like a sore thumb, so I knew they weren't from New Orleans.

I was left with Muni, and she was a lil' tipsy but she handled herself. I, on the other hand, had completely sobered up. She was the birthday girl and she felt too comfortable with the new niggas, so she had to have some type of connection and I wanted all the tea, especially the tall one with chocolate-covered skin with ocean blue eyes. He looked the calmest but deadliest of the three. His waist-length locs swayed from left to right as he walked. I had eyes on him when they first stepped inside the club. His bowlegs told a story of what he was carrying between his legs, and I wanted him to illustrate it to me. I wanted to feel that shit and before the night was over, I would. I couldn't wait to sit my ass on his face because he looked like he could eat a good wet pussy. He didn't give crazy vibes like the one Ye left with, but I knew it lurked somewhere in the shadows. There was a look of mystery in his eyes. I only saw him take two shots with his niggas but he smoked weed the rest of the time. The only time I didn't see him was when we were stepping and even then, I saw him, if that made sense. He wasn't hard to notice. Then with his red and white on, I knew he was a Kappa man. I can't say I ever had one of those. Kappa men were alpha males, or so I'd heard, and that was right up my alley because I was the submissive type. I looked around the party and didn't notice him, but I did see Mello. We made eye contact, and he headed in my direction. I tried to turn my head, but his heated gaze turned to rage and I couldn't look away. I knew he was looking for Ye, but I wouldn't sell my girl out because she deserved whatever she and Mad Max were about to get into.

"Where Ye went? It's time to head inside." He looked in my eyes trying to see if I would lie.

"The fuck you mean time to head inside? Ye is a grown ass woman, and this is our friend's party. You can leave if you want to, but my friend not going nowhere," I told him with attitude because that shit was starting to work my nerve. Yhental never went out, barely had a fucking life, and here he was acting like her father. "And yo' thot ass ain't going home, so why you tryna make her go?" I smirked at him.

"Girl, where the fuck is my sister?" he barked in my face and grabbed my arm. I knew Mello had a crush on me because I had one on him, but that was old news. We knew we couldn't cross that line, so the flirting was as far as that went. He got close to my face, and I didn't cower because I was one of the few people who wasn't scared of his overgrown ass.

"Minding her business, and you need to find you some," I

told him, standing on my toes to try and reach his height. I felt my arms being lifted in the air and looked behind me and noticed Muni trying to hold me up to his height. We both started laughing, and he couldn't help but to join in.

"Let Ye have her fun before y'all bring her back to the damn slave plantation," Muni said behind me, and I laughed harder, causing tears to come down my eyes. She let my arms go and stepped around me and inserted herself between us like she was the meat to our sandwich. She leaned over and whispered in his ear.

"You gon' save a dance for the birthday bitch?" I noticed she kissed the side of his neck. That was tea because I never knew that Muni liked him like that. He cowered under her spell, and I was at a loss for words. He looked down at her, devouring her with his eyes, and stepped back.

"I got more than just a dance for yo' fine ass." And just like that, Ye was forgotten. He palmed her ass, bringing them closer.

"Let my girl have fun and I'll come find you." She pecked his lips before turning away, grabbing my hand, and we went back up to her section that was on the second floor.

I can't lie, Muni was fine as fuck. She was a nice redbone with a thick body that I'd sampled from time to time. Her long hair swung down her back and her walk made all the niggas weak. We fucked around from time to time but still remained friends. We had a bond that could never be broken. I did feel a type of way with her and Mello's interaction, but I kept quiet. It wasn't jealousy, but I felt like the bitch was keeping secrets because she never told us about being that comfortable with him. Ye wouldn't care because she and I shared a different type of bond. Ye and I were friends first then I introduced the two, and we all had been stuck together since. Yes, I am bi-sexual and I live in my truth. Hell, Ye knew too because I was her first kiss. She may have told y'all she never been kissed before, but she left out the part about it being from a man. I taught her how to make a nigga's balls tingle just from a kiss. I hated that she was green to shit like that at her age, but it was what it was. I'd had my share of pussy in college, but Muni's was the best. When I wanted to dive in or fish in the sea, she was the only woman I called. However, tonight I wanted some dick, and I wanted it to come from tall, chocolate, and blue eyes that was sitting downstairs at the bar. I just hoped that Muni was related to them so she could tell me who he was. She better not play the jealousy card either, because we were having fun and we both weren't gay. From the way Mello damn near grabbed her pussy from the back, they had to be fucking. I'm surprised she liked his bully looking ass.

We sat down on the plush sofa and she threw me a sack of weed and a pack of Game Silvers so I could roll up. Muni pledged with us and we became sisters for life. Her name was Tardy because she couldn't be on time to shit, so it fit her perfectly. She poured the shots as I rolled the blunts. I lit the first one, inhaled, and chased it with a shot. I puffed off it a couple of times before passing it back to her, and she did the same.

"Before you talk yo' shit, what the fuck was that with Mello?" I asked, giving her the side eye. "Y'all some fucking familiar with each other. Let me find out you fucking that nigga." I chuckled a little to break the ice so she could tell me. I was on pins and needles to know the details about a dick I would never sample.

"I fuck with Mello, but I know how he gets down, so I stay my distance. I know the nigga don't want to be in a relationship so I keep my feelings on the back burner, but that plumber can lay the fucking pipe, bitch. I see why these bitches be pulling and scratching to get a taste of that nigga, but he don't wanna leave me alone." She put emphasis on me. "It's like when we together, he not the street nigga that these hoes know, he just regular ass Bakari. I'm trying not to catch feelings but sis, I don't know," she said, shaking her head, probably thinking about the way that nigga fucked her. He had her ass under a spell and she didn't even know it. I kind of felt sorry for her because I knew the type of dog ass nigga he was. He was going to break her heart, but she said she was protected so I wasn't about to make the shit my business. She passed the blunt back to me after I'd taken my shot, and I smoked. I started to feel the effects of this wicked ass combination. I was feeling myself but always handled myself like a lady.

"Enough about me and who I'm fucking, bitch, which one you got eyes for? Because I saw you looking. Ye got the monster and don't even know it yet, so I hope she know how to tame that nigga. Khamakazee is married, so you must want Khazeem," she said as I handed the blunt back to her. "Dreads and blue eyes, right?" she asked to confirm, but my smile was all the confirmation she needed. She had too much personal information on these niggas, so she had to be related to them in some way.

"And yes, they are my cousins from Atlanta and they are very possessive. The niggas in New Orleans ain't got shit on them." She laughed and choked on the blunt.

"What's Khazeem's story?" I asked her and took the blunt from her as she coughed up a lung.

"Ain't no story, bitch. My cousins run shit in Georgia. They are millionaires and can be very persuasive and deadly when provoked. Them niggas would have you thinking the fucking sky is pink when you know it ain't. They all love hard, especially Khazeem. Khaza, the one Ye left with, is the deadlier of the three, but he won't hurt her," she tried to convince me, but I wasn't worried because Mello and his army were only one phone call away. She leaned closer to me. "My aunt is the wicked witch of the west and will pump lead in yo' ass if you hurt her children, especially Khazeem," she spoke of them as if they were toddlers. "One last thing, Khazeem is a momma's boy and very clingy. All you gotta do is show his ass some genuine affection and he gon' fall in love with yo' ass and have the world at your feet," she said, and we both laughed. I was about to be a blessing and a curse because my love language was touch and clearly his was affection. I could do that effortlessly because it was in my nature, but this nigga might be crazy.

"Don't hurt my cousin, Nay, because my aunt would end you," she said with a seriousness in her voice that didn't scare me.

She was saying that shit like that was my intention. What if he hurt me, then what? She had to know there were repercussions if the situation was reversed. I didn't give a fuck who his mother was.

"Who gon' fall in love with who and who gon' hurt who and why the fuck are y'all so close together? Y'all kissing or some shit?" The bass and baritone in his voice caused my soul to stir. A slight tingle went up my spine with each word he spoke. This nigga was dangerous.

"Yo' nasty ass probably wanted us to be kissing but we weren't, pervert," Muni said, and we both laughed.

"So again, who gon' fall in love?" he asked, this time looking directly at me like I was transparent. I felt Muni hit my shoulder as I got lost in his eyes. I moved my hair to my right shoulder and matched his intense stare. I sat up straight with my back to the sofa and looked at him.

"You. I'mma make you fall in love with me," I told him with a cocky grin because I knew it was true. I winked my right eye at him and he blushed.

"Come on Khay, let's go downstairs and get a drink so you can check on your wife," I heard Muni say as she got up and walked past me, grabbing the other dude's arm and dragging him behind her, leaving me and Khazeem alone. He walked past me and sat next to me on the couch, and I wanted to jump on his fine ass. My pussy was on fire for him but something in my mind stopped me, told me that this was going to be something different, and I listened to it for once.

"Whatever you thinking about, don't do it because it ain't worth it," came out his mouth. "If you wanna fuck and let shit go, let's do that, but if you want to stick around for a while, I'm not going nowhere either. Pick your poison," he said as he picked up the blunt and relit it before inhaling it.

"What if I wanna do both?" I asked him, and he raised his eyebrow at me.

"That can be arranged as well." I don't know if it was the

weed mixed with the drink, but the way the words were coming out of his mouth went straight to my pussy. I was leaking like a faucet and I wanted him to drink from it. I picked up a paper plate and fanned myself with it. I felt the sweat forming on my top lip and fanned a little quicker.

"Come here." He curved his finger, signaling for me to come to him. I didn't know whether to move or not, so he took the liberty of grabbing my waist and sitting me in his lap. Both my knees were on each side of him with my coochie right on his dick. The only barrier between us were clothes. I felt his girth through my fabric and knew he was working with a monster. I looked into his eyes as he hit the blunt and held it in his mouth. His hands were on my cheeks, pulling my lips closer to his. He blew the smoke in my mouth, and I let it seep out my nose slow as hell. He pulled away and took the blunt from his lips and sat it down.

"That shit was sexy as hell, but what's your name, beautiful?" he asked, and I realized that I was practically on this man's dick, and he didn't even know my name. My cheeks flushed in embarrassment. I tried to put my head down, but his fingers lifted my chin up. I tried to remove myself from him, but he kept me in place with his hands on my ass cheeks.

"Nah, we both grown and the chemistry got me wanting to pull yo' fucking clothes off and fuck you right here, but I can tell you ain't on no fuck shit and neither am I," he said as he ran his hands up and down my back in a soothing manner. "Tell me yo' name," he whispered in my ear, making my thighs tighten.

"Nay," I said breathlessly as I started to grind against his dick. I didn't mean to but I couldn't help it. He leaned forward, grabbing the back of my neck.

"Nah, fuck a nickname. What's your real name?" His breath hitting my neck made the hairs on my back stand at attention. This nigga had my mind gone. He pulled me close to him, body to body.

"Nhairobe," I said and wrapped my arms around his neck as our lips met. Fireworks went off in my head as his tongue went down my throat for a sloppy kiss. The friction of our tongues touching and me dry humping him had me on the verge of squirting, but he stopped me.

"Nah, I ain't fucking you in a club, I got a house for that," he said, standing with me in his arms and walking toward the steps. My legs were around his back and my arms were around his neck as he carried me out the club and to his car. This was definitely about to be a night to remember.

Yhental

I didn't know what the fuck I was doing but whatever it was, I wanted to do it with him. It didn't matter what the future held because I was living in the moment. My mother would die ten deaths and Mello would paint the fucking city red if he knew that I had gotten in the car with a complete stranger. I felt free. I wasn't a caged bird under my mother and father's wing anymore. I didn't give a fuck if this nigga put me out his car in the middle of nowhere and left, I would be pleased. We hadn't said two words to each other, and that was fine with me because this was my car and it had a tracking device on it. I checked my phone and made sure my location was being shared with Nay so she would know where I was. I hoped she covered for me because I knew Mello would come looking for me.

"Don't overthink the shit. You chose to leave the club with a complete stranger and let him drive your car," he said as he got on the bridge. I looked over at him and laughed. He had a scowl on his face.

"I ain't overthinking shit. I'm just living in the moment," I answered back. "And smile. You look like you got a permanent scowl on your face, and you too handsome for that," I told him, but his face remained the same.

"I don't have shit to smile about," he said and turned his eyes back to the road. I was starting to think this was a bad idea. I should have followed my first mind and stayed at the club, but no, my half-drunk ass just had to see what the fucking hype was about. I was tired of being a virgin and hopefully, this mean ass nigga could change that tonight.

"Well, tell me what's wrong then," I told him as I reached over to rub the side of his tatted neck. I could almost bet he had tattoos everywhere on his body but his dick. He pulled away from my hand and continued to drive.

"You too fucking nosy, just sit there and enjoy your moment." He was being a sarcastic asshole, but I sat there and enjoyed the ride. I looked at his side profile and noticed he had a mole above his lip, and I touched it. He yanked his head to the side and swerved on the bridge.

"Watch yo' fucking hands Ye, before I bite them bitches off bruh, chill," he said and got back in the right lane. His shirt lifted a little and I noticed his gun. I wasn't scared because my brother and father carried them all the time. Nothing about him scared me, and that was strange. I felt a sense of peace even though he was being a mean jackass.

"You act like I was trying to slap yo' dumb ass. All I was trying to do was start a conversation with you," I told him, giving nothing but attitude. He glanced in my direction and laughed, but I didn't find shit funny.

"Ain't shit funny," I told him and mushed the side of his head.

"Keep yo' hands to yo' fucking self bruh, because if I get my lick back yo' ass gon' be crying, so chill," he said, still laughing at me.

"Oh, so you gon' hit me, Khaza?" I taunted him. This time his eyes grew lazy when he looked my way.

"Not the way you think I am." He winked his eye at me, and I blushed for the first time tonight.

"Say that shit again," he said, gripping the wheel tight. "My name sounds sexy as fuck rolling off yo' tongue," he continued and looked down at his dick. I could see the tent through his jeans.

"Not when yo' ass been being mean since we left the club," I told him, and he chuckled.

"I'm not mean love, I'm just careful," he said as he drove to the exit toward the business district.

He pulled into an underground garage at one of the upscale buildings in Downtown New Orleans. I barely came up this way because my father said it was a bad area, but he lied because it was lit up like the Las Vegas strip. He found an empty parking spot and parked. He hopped out the car and came to my side to open the door. I got out and he closed the door, pressing his body against mine. He grabbed my hands, putting them above my head against the top of my car. He pressed his forehead against mine and whispered, "You dripping in all this ice makes a nigga wanna fuck you with the lights off just to see that shit shine," he said into my lips like he was going to kiss me, but he didn't.

I felt my kitty come alive from his words. My clit jumped at the thought of the damage he could do to my body, but I was ready. I tried to put my arms around his neck, but his grip tightened, holding them hostage.

"Stop trying to keep control, Khaza. Let me have some." I lifted my head this time, kissing his top then bottom lip. I felt him stir in his jeans as a strained sound vibrated against my lips.

"You fucking with the wrong nigga, pretty girl. You too innocent to fuck with a nigga like me. I'mma fuck ya world up if you stay in mine for too long." He looked into my eyes then closed his and kissed my forehead. I felt every word he spoke run through my veins like fire, but I was willing to take that risk. I pushed my body up, making him move a little.

"What if I wanna be a part of your world?" I asked him, lifting my head so that our lips were inches apart.

"I tend to fuck shit up on my end, but if you wanna ride then don't get out when shit gets crazy." He pulled my body off the car to him, and we walked to the elevator and got inside. My mind was all over the place wondering what he meant by his words. He couldn't be that bad because he was an Omega. At least I knew he went to somebody's college. I would have to do more digging and ask more questions to get to know him, if he was willing to let me inside his head.

I stepped on the elevator and leaned with my back against the iron rail. I felt his eyes on my body, although I couldn't see them. He stood to the left side of me, pressing the number ten on the elevator before the door closed. It was silent for the first few minutes as I checked myself in the mirror in front of me. My makeup was still intact, and my outfit still looked like I'd just left the house. My hair was the same with a few loose strains of hair separated from my barrette. My ass was spilling out of the bottom of my romper and my hips looked extra wide. My heels were still on my feet but were killing them. I wanted to take them off, but I didn't want to be ghetto and walk the halls barefoot. I put my head down and chuckled to myself at the night's events that led to this very moment and sunk my teeth into my bottom lip. My mind went back to when I felt sexy as I stepped and danced with my line sisters as we popped and dipped to the music. I was lost in my thoughts, feeling free.

"Fuck it," I heard, and Khaza was in front of me before I could open my eyes. His hands on each side of my head against the wall as he stood close to me with the bottom half of his body dipped into mine.

"I know you gon' drive a nigga crazy, but I want that shit," he said, and his lips attacked my mine in a lust-filled kiss. He sucked my top then bottom lip while snaking his tongue against mine. He bent a little and my legs wrapped around his waist, and he hoisted me in the air. My hands were feeling all over his body as he kissed and sucked on my neck like it was his favorite flavor. One of his hands came down as he grabbed the front of my neck, sucking wherever there was skin out. I grinded against him because this was a new feeling to me. This shit was better than the rose Nay gave me on my birthday. He lifted me high enough so that my thighs were around his neck. He put his entire face against the fabric and sniffed.

"Even the pussy smells good. You gon' have a nigga willing to die behind you, Ye." Something about the way he said that had me on fire. Fuck the danger and seriousness behind his words. If he wanted to die, then let him fucking die. I pushed my covered pussy against face as he grabbed my ass cheeks, pulling me further into him.

"You want a nigga to eat this pussy?" he asked me, and I was on the verge of coming. My clit throbbed like a heartbeat as he kissed my inner thighs. He kissed the right one then looked up at me.

"Tell a nigga what you want me to do to this juicy motherfucker," he moaned, kissing my thigh again, and I whimpered like a wounded dog. I couldn't answer him. I was on a mental high that I didn't need to come down from. A high I wanted to chase forever. My mouth was dry from having it open for so long. Right when I felt the seat of my outfit get wet and my clit throb hard, he stopped. I mean, really fucking stopped. He let my body fall slowly to the floor, and I stood on wobbly legs. I tried to lean against him for leverage, but he pushed me away.

"Nah, I asked you a fucking question and you couldn't answer me? Just because my face was in yo' pussy? If you can't handle it with clothes on, I can only imagine how wild and psycho you would get if my tongue met yo' insides," he barked at me, and I knew this nigga was crazy. I ignored his attitude because there was a hint of lust that filled his eyes.

"You know what I wanted you to do but you stopped, so fuck it." I stood back against the wall, fixing my clothes. I felt his eyes on me, but I wouldn't look at him because if he wanted to play games, then they were about to begin.

"You talking mad shit, you couldn't even handle me with yo' ass in the air, so stop fronting like you living like that, because yo' pretty ass is not," he told me, and I raised my eyebrows at him. I was scared of what the night had in store for us, but I was definitely down to ride the night out. The elevator stopped on the tenth floor and we both walked out with me in front of him. I didn't have to look back to know that he was looking at my body. I knew he wanted me because it was in his eyes at the party. If he wanted to play hard to get, that was on him. I knew what I wanted and if he couldn't give it to me, then the next nigga would, but I wanted him. Something about his aura screamed danger, but I couldn't walk away. I was curious but I just hope that curiosity didn't kill this cat.

He got in front of me and led me to the living room. Everything in his place was different shades of blue. That was a turn on. Being that he was a Kappa turned me on even more. I sat on the sofa, and he sat next to me. I took a really good look at him. His skin was so smooth I could kiss and lick it all day long. He turned to look at me and licked his lips, and I thought about how they would feel covering my body with kisses. I crossed my legs at the thought.

"What yo' ass over there thinking about?" he asked me. I had false courage from somewhere because I answered him with the truth.

"About how your lips would feel all over my body."

He looked at me with slanted eyes. Eyes that held a hurt that I couldn't quite make out. He stared at me for a while before asking, "You want to smoke? Or shots?" He stared at my body from head to toe like I was naked. He made me feel transparent and caused goosebumps to fill my arms.

"I only smoke with my friends, but I guess I can put one in the air with you, and bring some shots too," I told him as he got up to get what I asked for. He came back with two blunts and shot glasses with a bottle of D'ussé. He must have been paying close attention to me at the club, because that was all I drank. He poured the shots, and I took one while he lit the blunt and smoked. I could tell the weed was taking effect because his eyes got low and red.

"Come here." He nodded his head to me. I guess I didn't

move fast enough because he grabbed my waist and pulled me on top of him. With a thigh on each side of him, I settled on his lap, right on top of his dick. "Open ya mouth," he told me, and I did. He put the blunt in his mouth, inhaled, and then blew the smoke out, covering my entire face, giving me a shotgun. When our lips touched, I didn't want to pull away, but I had to. I inhaled the smoke through my mouth and let it slowly leave my mouth and nose at the same time. He looked at me and smiled while grabbing the front of my throat, pulling me in for a kiss. He slid his tongue in my mouth and I sucked on it. I couldn't let him know that I wasn't the best kisser, so I followed his lead. When he sucked my lips, I sucked his. I wrapped my arms around his neck, pulling him in deeper. He leaned forward with me still on him and poured us another shot. This time he threw his back but kept mine in his hand. He put the blunt to my mouth and I toked it, holding the smoke there while he poured the shot down my throat.

"That shit was so sexy." He pulled me back to him, kissing the base of my throat. My body was on fire as I moved against him to release some of the friction that was causing a dull ache between my thighs. He grabbed my hips to stop my movements.

"Nah, stop while you ahead because you ain't ready for me, Ye." He moaned my name like it tasted good in his mouth.

"You don't know what I'm ready for, Khaza," I told him, and he stared hard at me.

"What's your real name?" he asked me, and I was caught off guard.

"Yhental," I told him breathlessly as I tried to kiss him, but he stopped me.

"What type of name is that?" he asked me.

"The type of name my mother gave me," I told him.

"Why you want to fuck me so bad, Yhental?" he asked me, and I didn't have an answer. I couldn't tell him I was a virgin because I didn't know how the nigga was going to react.

"Because you sexy as fuck and I want you," I told him because it was the truth.

"You don't even know me though," he told me, and I frowned. He was giving me a hard fucking time like our genders were reversed. He had me second guessing leaving with him if all he was going to do was interrogate me. I sat back to really look at him.

"Tell me about you then," I told him since he wanted to be so fucking talkative.

"I'm from Atlanta, Georgia." He kissed my lips. "I have two brothers." Another kiss this time with a little tongue. "I graduated with my master's in psychology and got my PhD." He grabbed my hips, making me grind against him. "I'm a Kappa man, as you know." He kissed the left side of my neck, torturing me. "And I came to New Orleans to get away from some shit back home that I ain't discussing because I don't trust you yet," he said, kissing and sucking the other side of my neck. My clit jumped as he rubbed my breasts through the material I was wearing.

"What do you do for a living?" I asked him, kissing his lips.

"Nothing that concerns you" he answered, and I didn't give a fuck what he did for a living. He looked like money, so I knew he had a lot of it. That shit didn't excite me because I came from money. I nodded my head in agreement because right now, this moment was all that mattered. He stood to his feet with me in his arms. I wrapped my legs around his waist as he carried me to what I assumed was his bedroom. He threw me on the bed, and I sat up with my feet dangling to the floor.

"Take this shit off now," he told me, but it didn't register what the fuck he was saying. He got on his knees and reached around my neck to unhook my halter top. He let it fall and my breasts sat up with my nipples pointed at him.

"Damn," he moaned to himself as he continued to explore my body. His soft yet rough hands ran down my tummy and pulled at my bottoms. "Lift up, but keep those heels on," he said, and I lifted my hips for him to take my entire outfit off. Once it was removed and he threw it across the room, I scooted my butt back in the bed until I was in the middle. I let my legs gap open to show him the juice that seeped from my opening.

"You tryna tease a nigga and shit," he said as he pulled his shirt over his head and stepped out his jeans, leaving him in just his boxers. He still had the blunt in his hand as he crawled between my legs, resting on top of me.

"Hit this." He put the blunt to my lips and I inhaled. I blew the smoke in his face, and he ate that shit up. He finished the blunt, putting it in the ashtray that sat on his nightstand. I came back to me and looked in my eyes.

"I know I'mma be fucked up after this, and don't ask why because you wouldn't understand," he told me, and I kept my mouth closed.

He licked me from my forehead to my lips and neck. He then flipped me over on my stomach, and I arched my back. He licked from the top to the bottom of my spine and kissed my sides and hips in between. My body trembled. I knew he felt it, and he blew on my back. I had lost all control of my body and gave it to him. I felt like I was in a movie. There was no way that my body should feel like this. The shit felt unreal. My entire body was throbbing and there was nothing I could do about it. I shouldn't even be fucking with this grown ass man with my inexperienced ass, but here I was playing with fire. He kissed both my ass cheeks before flipping me back over on my back.

"Bust them legs open for me." My legs fell open from his words, but I guess that wasn't enough. He pressed the inside of my thighs until my knees were pressed against the bed. Thank God I was flexible. "Pussy just wet for a nigga." He brought his face to my inner thighs, and I thought I was going to pass the fuck out. I tried to throw my pussy in his face, but he backed up.

"Patience, tell me what you want me to do with this pussy," he said, staring into my eyes.

"Eat it." I didn't recognize my own voice. He kissed my inner left thigh then my right, causing my body to vibrate. He was torturing me. He was kissing everywhere but the one place I needed him to touch the most. I felt my wetness seeping down the crack of my ass as he blew on my clit.

"Ahhhhh," I screamed as his lips attacked my clit. My back arched off the bed as he devoured my insides. I felt his tongue inside of me, and I started to flow like a river.

"Did I tell you to wet my face yet?" he asked me, and I couldn't answer. My clit jumped with every word he spoke. I shook my head from left to right.

"Well, why the fuck did you nut then?" he asked me before his tongue met my asshole. I was glad that I took Nay up on her offer to get waxed earlier today while we were out. I tried to squeeze my ass cheeks together, but that only made him lick harder.

"Open them cheeks up and let me in," he said, and I relaxed. He sucked and licked on my asshole until I was about to nut again.

"Don't fucking do it, Ye, without my permission," he said, and I tried my best to hold my nut. He went from one hole to the next, driving me crazy. My hands twirled my nipples, sending me into a sexual frenzy.

"Nut now," he hummed in my pussy, and I let go and creamy liquid flowed out me like a river and didn't stop. I felt like I was nutting forever. He sucked it all up and waited until my body wasn't trembling and calmed down before standing up.

"You good?" he asked me with a smirk on his face that was now etched in my memory. My throat was dry, and I couldn't answer him. He kneeled back down and opened my legs up. I felt his finger trying to penetrate my walls, but he was met with some resistance and my body tensed. I tried to play it off, but he caught on quick. He stood to his feet and looked down my body.

"You a fucking virgin?!" he barked so loud that I knew the entire building heard him. I felt embarrassed, like the whole fucking world knew. I was scared to answer him because of the scowl that was on his face. He pulled my ankles to him before I could crawl to the head of the bed.

"Answer me, Yhental!" he yelled again, and it pissed me off.

"Is that a fucking problem?" I stood to my feet, getting into his personal space. "Because it wasn't a fucking problem when yo' face was just in there," I continued my rant as he ran his hands over his head.

"I fucking knew this shit was too good to be true. You ain't even gotta answer that because the fact that my fucking finger couldn't get past your hymen confirmed it," he yelled in my face, and I pushed him away from me. I felt humiliated. I wanted to crawl into a hole and die. My entire fantasy was turning into a nightmare right before my eyes.

"Yes, I am a fucking virgin, but I don't go around telling every nigga that wanna fuck with me that," I yelled in his face, and he grabbed the front of my throat in a sexual way.

"Man, fuck the next nigga because ain't no more niggas after me unless you want them dead. You better hope I don't kill the niggas before me," he said so close to my face that I could smell my essence on them. "Why the fuck would you leave with me when you knew you were a fucking virgin, man?" he asked me like I had the fucking answer.

"I can't fuck with you. I'm a dirty ass nigga and I don't deserve your virginity, Yhental." Now I was confused because first it was he gon' kill every nigga behind him, but yet he didn't want to fuck with me. My feelings were crushed, but I didn't know why because I didn't even know this nigga. Each word that came out his mouth popped a heart string that I didn't know I had.

"You gotta get the fuck out," he yelled at me, picking up my clothes and throwing them at me. He gave me a look of disgust, and I hurried to put my clothes on. "Coming in here with virgin pussy. I should have smelled that shit from a mile away." He was making my anger rise.

"You must like to fuck hoes, and I'm not that," I told him and yanked my purse and keys out his hand. I look at him one last time before walking to his front door. I thought that he would try to stop me, but he didn't. I opened the door and walked out to get on the elevators. I looked back at him as he stood in the hallway, looking like he wanted to stop me, but his feet or mouth wouldn't move. I turned back around and got on the elevator, and it was in my car that I beat the fucking the steering wheel for being so stupid to think that he would want a girl like me. I pulled off after my five minutes of crying and drove home, praying that my mother or father weren't at the door waiting on me. This was the first time I had let the sun beat me home, and I wasn't proud of it at all.

I pulled up to my house and thankfully, all the lights were off. The butler took my keys, and I stepped in the house removing my shoes. I held them in my hand as I went to my room and closed the door. It was then I realized that I didn't have my phone, but I wasn't going back to his home to get it. I couldn't even call Nay and tell her what happened. I would just tell my daddy to get me another one later. I dragged myself to the shower and then got in my bed to go to sleep and pretend this day never happened.

Bakari

I didn't know where the fuck Ye was, but I hoped she was safe. I tried calling her phone, but it kept going straight to voicemail. I even tried to pull up her location, but it was off. I wanted to send Piper to find her but I'd just let it be because she deserved to be free and not cooped up in the house all day. After Nay left with some nigga with funny-colored eyes, Muni walked downstairs to the bar with another nigga. He stepped away outside the club and I walked over to her. I could tell she was feeling herself because her eyes were low as fuck and red. I walked behind her as she stood at the bar, placing my palms on each side of the counter, blocking her from getting away. I kissed the side of her neck and heard her hiss. She moved her hair out the way so I could get better access, and I bit then sucked her skin, leaving a mark.

"I'm ready for my dance, pretty girl." I looked at our reflection in the mirror and smiled lazily. If I ever wanted to settle down, it would be with her without a doubt, but the hoe in me wouldn't let me be with just one woman. It was something about a hood rat bitch that turned a nigga on, but Muni was the exception. She was the only good girl I ever turned out, and I didn't regret it. She pushed her thick ass against my dick and her head fell back against my chest. The smell of her hair made the hairs on my back stand up. I already knew she was coming home with me.

"Of course, I am, Daddy," she told me, and the DJ dropped Vedo's "Face Down" as we made our way to the dance floor.

You know my body, yeah (what?)
Your ex nigga, I'm not (hmm)
You pop that freak shit on the phone
Just wait 'til I get back home, oh, yeah
You gon' try to run from it but
You gotta stay and don't let down
I'ma make you take it all this time
When I bend that ass down
You say it's all mine and it's up to me
Girl, this is all that I need
I want you face down, ass up
On all fours
Girl, you can scream all night long
Girl, I want you to myself

I grabbed her body, pulling her close to mine. My arms around her waist, her arms around my neck. We moved in sync with the music. She circled her pussy against me, and my dick rose for the occasion. She held on to me like she never wanted to let me go, and I felt that shit. This was our moment. Nothing mattered but us. This was the first time I'd ever shown PDA with a female. I heard her humming the words to the song as I kissed her neck. That led to me kissing her lips. She slid her tongue into my mouth and for a moment, we forgot where the fuck we were. I palmed her ass, making her dress rise, but I didn't give a fuck. She had me right where she wanted me. I was in full lust mode and if she didn't stop grinding on me, I was gon' fuck her right there on the dance floor. She turned around, putting her ass on my dick as the second verse played.

You gon' try to run from it but
You gotta stay and don't let down
I'ma make you take it all this time
When I bend that ass down
You say it's all mine and it's up to me
Girl, this is all that I need (I need)
I want you face down, ass up
On all fours (all fours)
Girl, you can scream all night long
Girl, I want you to myself (ooh-ooh, woah, oh-oh)
Oh, baby
Things that you do drive me crazy
I want you all to myself (all to myself)

Vedo spoke every word to her that my voice couldn't speak. I wanted her all to myself and she knew it, but I couldn't leave the streets alone. With her back against my chest, she winded her wide hips against me making my dick brick. I walked her over to the nearest dark corner. I grabbed her wrists, putting them above her head with one of my hands. I pulled her dress up to her waist and fumbled with my jeans to get my dick out.

"Just let me put the tip in then we can leave," I whispered in her ear as I kissed her exposed back. I held my dick in my hand and bent a little to her height to slide right in. This was the first time I felt her without protection, and I was hooked. Her warm, tight walls swallowed my shit. I bit into my bottom lip to force myself not to nut. I hadn't even started moving yet, and I knew if I did it would be over before it could start. I pulled my dick out of her and put it up. I turned her around to kiss her and whispered, "We gotta get the fuck outta here," and smiled before leading the way outside the club to my car.

ONE WEEK LATER

It had been one week since I took Muni to my condo, and I held her hostage ever since. I turned her and my phones off because we didn't need no distractions. We had been fucking like rabbits all over my condo since that night. The only time we weren't fucking was when I ordered food, or we tapped out. Now we were laying face to face, staring at each other. It was one of those rare moments when she wanted to talk.

"What's on yo' mind, Muni? You been quiet for too long," I told her, pulling her closer to me because she was too far away.

"Nothing. I'm just trying to keep my distance because I know you like dust buckets, and I ain't trying to get my heart broken," she told me honestly, and I felt that.

"You know my intentions are not to hurt you in any way, but you know the type of nigga you fucking with," I told her, because we agreed when we first started fucking around a year ago that we wouldn't keep secrets from each other.

"I know that, but I'mma need you to keep that same energy if you see me with another nigga," she said, and my eyebrows curled.

"Nah, that ain't gon' happen. You ain't trying to lose yo' life behind no outside dick. This pussy belongs to me," I told her, palming her pussy through the sheets. "You know I don't take them hoes nowhere. That ain't how I roll," I told her, and it was the truth. The hoes I fucked every day of the week didn't get outside treatment.

"We didn't use protection, Bakari." She covered her mouth with her hand, but it was too late to think about that now.

"Fuck, we both clean and you on birth control, right?" I asked her, and she nodded her head up and down because we both didn't want kids right now.

"Don't worry about them hoes because they gon' always be there just to get clout, but I want you here forever." I didn't recognize my own voice as I said it. I noticed her cheeks turned red, but she knew I would never lie to her.

"I ain't got time to worry about a hoe and what you doing with them, long as that shit don't make it to my front door," she told me, and I pulled her on top of me. She was making a nigga's dick hard barking out orders like that. She mounted me and sat straight on my dick with no assistance. She began to bounce up and down in slow motion, making my toes curl. This wasn't fucking. She was making love to me, and I was enjoying every minute of it. Muni had my fucking mind gone. I was missing out on handling my street business to just be with her.

"Ride this dick like it's yours," I coached her as I grabbed her titties. The shit was becoming too intense, so I sat up and gripped her hips, making her grind harder and faster.

"Fuck." I felt my face frown as I kissed her chin then her neck. Her head came down to mine as she sucked my tongue.

"I'll kill any nigga that touch this pussy after me," I told her, feeling outside my body.

"You make sure don't no other bitch ride yo' dick like this," she said back, making my dick harder. I knew with her riding me like this I was about to nut quick.

"There's only one you, Muni," I told her as I let my load off deep inside her. She fell to the side of me exhausted. She had drained all the energy I had left in my body with that nut. She turned to her side and looked at me like she was in love, which she probably was.

"I'm taking you out today," I told her without making eye contact. I lifted her from the bed and carried her to the shower bridal style.

After another round in the shower, we washed each other and got out. I gave her one of Ye's new maxi dresses because they were the same size, but Ye was a little shorter so the dress was shorter on her. I planned to take her to Oakwood to get her some stuff because she wasn't leaving me no time soon. I also needed to stop at the Apple store to get her an iPad so she could catch up on her reading while I was out handling business. Once we were dressed, we left out the door and hopped in the car headed to the mall.

Once we were parked, I went around to open her door for her to step out. We walked in the mall and went straight to Dillard's. She needed clothes, bras, and panties, and I needed more Polo boxers. After I got what I needed, I went to find her. I found her going through the racks of clothes, grabbing the shit she needed. I walked up behind her and kissed her neck, and she giggled but continued to shop.

"Oh, I see he brings his hoes out now, and he likes them young." I knew that voice anywhere, but I wasn't for the drama, so I hoped like hell that Muni didn't hear her. Tasha was the one bitch that I wished I could unfuck. She thought just because I gave her chump change that she had rank in my life, but she didn't. I gave all my hoes money to keep them away from me unless I wanted pussy or mouth. If they couldn't follow my rules, then I cut them off. I ignored what she was saying to her flunkies and continued to kiss on Muni. I heard her steps getting closer, and I knew it was about to be some shit.

"Then the nigga likes to rob the fucking cradle," she said louder, causing her girls to laugh louder. I knew Muni heard her because her head tilted a little bit, but she ignored it.

"Control your hoe, Bakari," I heard Muni mumble under her breath. Tasha didn't know that Muni had some dogs on her, and it didn't take much to flip her switch.

"Mello, I know—" Tasha couldn't get another word out before Muni was turning around to face her. I grabbed her arm, but she yanked away from me, rolling her eyes.

"Bitch, go ahead before I unleash my pit bull on you." I looked down at Muni, and we both started laughing. Tasha was a fucking joke and the sooner she realized that, the better off we all would be.

"Bae, it's cool, I got you. Never stoop to the peasants' level when you're standing with your queen," she said, kissing my lips then turning to face Tasha.

"I didn't know Mello fucked with the help," Muni told her, and that shut her ass up. "And no, hunni, he ain't robbing the cradle but fucking a bitch like you, he was definitely fucking somebody's grandmother. Come on, Mello, before I punch the fuck outta yo' granny who can't stay in her lane." She grabbed the front of my shirt and walked us to the nearest counter to check out.

"You know you fuck some ugly bitches, but the next time she feel the need to make her presence known, I'mma unleash these hands on her," she told me as I paid for our stuff so we could leave. As we walked to the car, I gave her, her phone and turned on mine. I had missed calls from Big B and I knew he was about to rip me a new asshole. I dialed his number, and he picked up on the first ring.

"Bring yo' ass here nigga, and bring Muni's fast ass with you. Don't think I don't know you fucking her," he said and disconnected the call before I could get a word in. We put the shit in the car and headed to my parents' house.

After 20 minutes of driving, we pulled up through the gate. I pulled up and hopped out the car as the butler opened the door for Muni. I handed him my keys to go park my car as me and her headed inside. Once inside the door, we took off our shoes because that was a rule in their home. That was a rule that I didn't miss at all. We walked in the foyer, and I could smell the famous Yaki Mein that my mother cooked when she was in a good mood. Either Pops dicked her down or something good was happening on her favorite soap opera. My father met us before we could make it to the kitchen.

"Bakari, I need to speak to you in private, and Muni, you go upstairs and talk to Ye because she been crying since the night of your party. I had to get her ass a new phone because she claimed she lost the original one. She won't tell me what the fuck happened, but all she comes out her room for is to eat, then it's back up there to her room. She won't even talk to your momma," he said, and Muni excused herself upstairs to the room. I followed my father down to his mancave as he closed and locked the door.

"I see why you turned yo' fucking phone off and been MIA for the past week," he said soon as I sat down on his sofa.

"What the fuck was that in the mall, Bakari?" he asked me, and I was shocked. He must've had one of his men following me or some shit. "I'll say this one time only. Stop fucking with them hood rat, CNA working bitches because they gon' be your downfall. Leave those rats in the gutter where they belong before they drag you with them," he said, giving me a stern look.

"I didn't know that Tasha and her dust buckets were gonna be there. I haven't fucked with Tasha in a while, Pops," I told him.

"Yo' ass is lying. You just fucked her a week ago, but you'll learn one day. Love the one who loves you first, not the one that's in love with the thought of loving you," he told me, and I changed the subject because I didn't want to hear that shit. Tasha was canceled before that shit in the mall. Her actions furthermore confirmed why I didn't want to fuck with her anymore.

"Moms must be in a good mood to be cooking Yaki Mein, huh?" I asked him with a side eye. Yaki Mein was a mixture of spaghetti with chunks of beef and green onions with different spices along with boiled eggs and sometimes shrimp.

"Yeah, I dicked her down last night and she woke up in a better mood," he said, and we both laughed. "But that's not why I called you down here," he said, and I sat up.

"Piper came to me with some shit about some new niggas trying to blend in with our city, and I ain't feeling it. Something about the Montiago Mafia. I looked them up, but the only thing they are connected to is resorts with hotels and shit but no pictures of the owners. They hiding behind something and I need to find out," he said as I listened, "We don't need no unnecessary beef with some niggas that don't belong here or trying to take over, so we dead that shit before it even starts. Then came the shit with yo' sister and that fact that she don't wanna tell me is making me want to revert back to my old ways and paint the fucking city red," he said and sat next to me.

"Did you get the video footage from the club that night?" I

asked him. He pulled his MacBook. He opened it up and pulled up the video from that night. I watched the footage and noticed Ye leave with the same nigga that defended her from a nigga dancing on her, but I didn't get his name. I knew he was with two other niggas that were very familiar with Muni, but I wasn't gon' tell my pops that. The way the camera was angled, you couldn't see their faces anyway. I was about to go upstairs and drag Muni out the room to see what the fuck she knew but decided against it, because that would start some shit between me and Ye. I knew she told her girls everything, especially Nay, but didn't tell me shit. I would cover for her, but when it came to her safety from these niggas in the street, it was time for trial and I was the fucking judge.

"I need to put some foot soldiers to the ground to see who the fuck these niggas are and where they came from," I told my daddy and got up to walk out the basement.

I walked into the kitchen where my mother was stirring the big pot of food. I kissed her cheeks as she turned to me.

"Chu better know what you doing messing with chu sista friend. Muni is good girl," she said in broken English. I didn't understand after all these years of being in the United States and she still could speak proper English.

"Momma, I am not going to hurt Muni. We are both adults and we know what we are doing," I said to her, and she turned around to finish cooking.

"Set the table, Bakari," she said, and I went in the cabinet to get the plates and utensils to set the table. I even made an extra setup for Muni.

Nhairobe

"Damn, Khazeem," I moaned out as I rode his dick nice and slow. I had been laid up with him since the night I left with him from Muni's party. He took me back to his home. What started out as us getting to know each other and talking turned me into a raging inferno, and I had to feel him. Since Muni told me what he liked, I was adamant on making him mine.

If we weren't fucking, we were eating and talking, getting to know each other. He told me about being from Georgia and coming this way with his brothers to expand his business. I told him about my education, but he didn't need to know where I laid my head at because it was embarrassing. I didn't want him to know I lived in the slums. He told me he graduated from Clark Atlanta University with his master's in business administration with a minor in accounting. At the age of twenty-eight, he was a very powerful man. His demeanor exuded it. He handled all the money for his family's chain of hotels and resorts named Montiago Heat. He stated that they had locations from California to Washington, even one on the Las Vegas strip. They were looking to open a location in the business district in New Orleans. That was cool. I told him about me leaving and going to Spelman with Ye in January for school, and he smiled like a proud parent. I already knew about his maw from Muni, but I wanted to see what he had to say about her. He told me that he was a momma's boy, and that was fine with me long as they had boundaries. This nigga had daddy money.

"Fuck Nay, you killing me," he said as I picked up my speed. Another thing I noticed about him was that he liked to be in control but hated to lose control. There was a very thick barrier between the two. Me being on top of him was making him slowly lose control. He sat up and started to fuck me back before flipping us over with me on all fours. I arched my back deep as he slapped my ass, making it jiggle. I twerked my ass cheeks as he slid back inside me. He wanted to beat the pussy up but, in this position, I still had control. I raised up on my toes higher and started moving slower and in a circle.

"You gon' make me nut too soon, Nay, baby please," he begged, but I didn't stop. I felt his tongue lick my spine and that made me go slower. I felt his legs trembling and knew he was close, but I didn't stop. I was going to make love and fuck him until he came. I felt his dick throbbing inside of me and knew he was about to drop a heavy load. I pulled him out of me and turned around so he could shoot his warm cream all over my face.

I loved Khazeem's house. It was made of glass. Wherever a wall was, on the inside it was mirrors. Everywhere we made love we saw our reflection, and that only heightened my senses. I never watched myself being fucked or fucking someone before, so that was a first. He slapped his dick on my mouth until all his nut was gushing out.

"I think I'm love with yo' ass after this shit," he said, and I smiled with a nut-filled face.

"That's the plan, baby," I told him before getting off the bed and going to the bathroom for a warm towel. I came back in the room, and he was turning his phone on. I cleaned him off and went to put the towel away. I got back in the sheets with him, and he was the first to start talking.

"I don't want this shit to ever end," he told me, staring in my eyes, and I hoped he meant it.

"Only we control our actions, baby," I told him, bringing his face to mine for a kiss. I slithered my tongue in his mouth like a thick python and groaned when his phone rang. I broke the kiss and turned my head because I didn't want to be in his business. He reached over and grabbed my chin, turning my head back.

"Don't do that. I will not start whatever we got going on with a lie. I am a single man, and this is my mother calling me," he said, turning the screen to me so I could see. I kissed his lips then worked my way down to his nipples. I wished I could kiss his fucking irises because they were so beautiful. I got on top of him and slid down his body as his phone rang in his hand. When he realized what I was about to do, he tried to pull my head up, but it was too late. One of his balls was in my mouth. He groaned with his hands in my hair.

"Answer the phone, baby." I sucked his other ball, and he lifted a little to get comfortable. My hands were sliding up and down his shaft until I could get my mouth to it.

"Ssssss, fuck," he said, looking down at me, and that hiss activated my superfreak powers.

"Ya Ma." His voice was strained as my tongue licked the veins that protruded from his shaft.

"Khazeem, I know you didn't answer the phone while you fucking some ghetto bitch down there," she yelled in his ear, and I heard her. That made me deep throat him even harder. When his tip touched the back of my throat, I hummed to make him moan.

"What's up, Ma, you calling me too early with this." He tried to hide his moans, but I would let him. He gave me a heated look. He dropped his phone to the side of him on the bed.

"I don't know what lil' bitch you got sucking yo' lil' dick, but don't play with me, Khazeem. I'll take the next flight out and be at your front door," she yelled, and we didn't realize she was on speaker.

"Ma, chill, what's up? I'm listening to you." He wasn't because his eyes were rolling to the back of his head.

"Hang the phone up, Khazeem," I said loud enough for his maw to hear. I had his mind and body, and momma bird should have hung up before she heard her son screaming like my bitch. Every time I felt his dick throb, I suctioned my cheeks to stop the throbbing and he was losing it.

"Put her ass on the fucking phone since she wants to tell you to hang up on me." He tried to grab the phone, but I was quicker and kept it on speaker with a mouth full of dick.

"Good morning, mother-in-law," I told her, pausing at the tip of his dick, driving him insane as his bucked out his head. "The name calling is really childish, but my name is Nhairobe and I'll be around for a while, so have a seat and wait your turn, and what's your name?" I told her, massaging his balls, waiting for her to answer.

"Khaya," she said with a different tone.

"Well, I'm your new and only daughter-in-law. And just a word of advice, I can give him something you won't be able to give him, and that's this mouth and pussy, so scoot hunni, because there is a new sheriff in town," I told her as I spit on his dick, letting my saliva connect from my mouth to his mushroom head. Khazeem was frustrated. He didn't know whether he wanted to hang up the phone and get his nut or get his nut while his mother listened. The choice was his because I wasn't stopping.

"Give Khazeem the phone, child," she said sarcastically before I put the phone on mute and gave it to him.

"Please babe, let me talk to my momma." He tried to push my head away, but I told him no.

"This my dick and I was gon' suck it whether she was on the phone or in our presence. Now move yo' fucking hands and talk," I told him, and he put the phone to his ear, but I stopped him.

"No, keep her on speaker so I can hear what she tells you," I told him, and he unmuted the phone. I remembered Muni telling me that Khaya was a firecracker, but I was the bitch holding the flame.

"I'm here, Ma," he told her while my head bobbed up and down his dick.

"Am I on speaker?" she asked, and I looked at him shaking my head no, making him squirm like a fish.

"No Ma." I had him lying to his momma already. This pussy and mouth got a whole lotta power in it.

"Whoever this woman is that you are messing with, you better let her know what's up with me. On another note, I like her. Don't fuck this up. She got spice and I like that. When I come out there, make sure she's with you so I can put a face to my new daughter-in-law." She laughed before hanging the phone up. I sucked faster and faster as he chased his nut and fucked my face until his nut shot to the back of my throat. He growled until he emptied every drop into my mouth, and I licked it all up.

"You a bad fucking woman to talk to my mother like that," he told me, pulling me to him to kiss my lips and taste my handywork.

"Nah, I'm just a woman who won't tolerate disrespect from a nigga or a bitch," I told him and grabbed my phone. I looked down at it and had over twenty-five missed calls and text messages from Ye and the most recent from Muni. I knew she left with Mello, so I wondered what the fuck she wanted. Then I thought back to what the fuck Muni told me about Khaza. I flipped my phone in Khazeem's face.

"Does yo' brother have something to do with the times my best friend called me over the course of the time we been together? Did you talk to him?" I sat up in the bed to look at him.

"I talked to the nigga the other day, but he didn't mention Ye," he told me, and I believed him.

I got out the bed and put a pair of his basketball shorts on and one of his shirts before sliding my feet into his oversized slippers and grabbed my purse. He rushed behind me, grabbing me by my waist and whispering my ear, "Where you going? I wasn't ready for you leave me yet," he said like a lovesick puppy.

"I gotta go check on my friend to make sure she straight, then I'm going home to change," I told him.

"Just let me take you then," he said, and I thought about where I lived and declined. I could have been moved out the St. Thomas project because I had more than enough money to do so, but I chose to stay because it was all I knew. I was immune to piss-smelling hallways and stairs. The crackheads that greeted me every morning when I got to the front of the building. It gave me a sense of peace to be surrounded by the same crackheads I'd grown to love and know. It's crazy, but it was my life and I wasn't ready for him to see that side of me because it was too early.

"I'll take that answer as a no, so why don't you take my Range Rover and bring it back when you finish." He thought he was slick. Nigga with money like he had had tracking devices on everything, but I'd let him have that one because I wanted to see him later, and I always wanted to drive a Range. He went back to the room and brought back the key fob. I kissed his lips and walked outside to go and check on my friend.

When I pulled up to Ye's house, I was let in by the butler. I walked straight in, spoke to her parents, and went to her room. I walked in and she was balled up on her bed facing the window.

"Ye, I'm here babes, what's wrong?" At the sound of my voice she got up and looked at me with bloodshot eyes. I held her in my arms as she cried and told me what happened the night she left the club with Khaza.

Khaza

Fuck, fuck, fuck. I knew I had fucked with Ye, but that wasn't my intention. I had a hard time expressing my feelings, and I blamed my mother for that shit. Since I was a kid all she taught me was how to hate. She loved on us hard but when it came to women, she told us that they were poison. All they wanted was to fuck us for clout and leave us high and dry. She never told us about the good girls that were left on this side of the earth, and I may have fucked over one of those. It had been a week since I put Ye out and I was feeling that shit. Now I saw how women felt when their hearts were broken. I couldn't eat, couldn't sleep, I couldn't even fucking function because of what I'd done. She caught me off guard with the virgin shit, and I didn't know how to react. I didn't want to be the reason for her first heartbreak because I was sure to break it. I wasn't taught how to properly love someone so I couldn't love anyone but my brothers and Khaya.

I couldn't sulk in my misery because business still had to be taken care of. I went to Florida and got the 18-wheeler full of weapons and parked it by Khazeem. I had my tailor fly in from Georgia for my Gucci suit and Ferragamos. Today was a good day as I got dressed to meet the realtor who I was buying the warehouse with. It was a three-story building that was a great steal. I talked her into selling the building for 500 thousand and I'd thrown an extra 100K in there for her and her time. I was there on time with the signed paperwork and bag of money to cover everything, plus a bonus for her getting me the building so quick. I'd run into her in the jewelry store on Canal Street while I was out buying all types of shit for Ye. I would give it to her eventually if she ever came back around. I thought she would have realized that she left her phone at the house and came back for it, but she probably got another one just to not see my face again. I couldn't blame her because I was harsh to her. Every day since she left, I replayed that scene in my head over and over again. I felt like I didn't deserve her. She was too good for me because I was a monster, and I couldn't change that because it was a part of who I was. I couldn't always hide behind the hotels and resorts because I also sold weapons for a living, legal and illegal. Once, my mask fell off and my real face displayed, she would be hurt, and that's the last thing I wanted to do to her.

I looked down at my Rolex and realized that the bitch was running late. She jumped at the chance to sell me the property but was late for the closing. I sat down in the chair, shaking my leg waiting for her to show up. After 20 more minutes of waiting, I heard the door creak open. I stood and turned around, and there she was but with the nigga I saw at the club. That was strange because I thought he was fucking with my cousin Muni, but maybe shit was different. Either way, I was going to tell her, or this nigga was going to lose his life for fucking over her. He extended a hand to me and I gave him a firm handshake. I knew he was related to Ye, but I would wait to see if he remembered me.

"Bakari," he said, "and this is my bitch, Tasha. She told me about somebody buying this building and I decided to accompany her to the closing," he offered information that I didn't ask for. Strike two. The first one was being with this female knowing he fucked with Muni. Either he really didn't know who I was, or he was a great fucking actor. Maybe Ye didn't tell him what happened between us. It didn't matter because I was always strapped, waiting for something to pop off.

"I signed the paperwork, and the money is over there in the duffle bag," I said more to her than him, and I didn't miss his smirk. That confirmed that he knew exactly who I was. They walked over to the table, and I was behind them because I didn't trust them to walk in front of them. He picked up the bag and noticed it was heavy.

"Bag a lil' heavy, huh?" he asked, and I looked at him.

"Do I look like a nigga that carries light shit?" I asked him, and Tasha stepped in.

"Okay, Mr. Montiago, I'll process your paperwork and I'll email you everything," she said as they left the way they came in. I waited until they were gone to go to my car. I hopped in and revved my engine, when I cellphone rang. I looked at the screen noticing that it was my mother on the line.

"What's up, Ma?" I asked, surprised that she called me and not her golden child, Khazeem. Then again, I'm not surprised because she only called me when she wanted someone killed.

"Hey baby, come pick me up from the airport." I rolled my eyes to the ceiling because I knew her impromptu visit would give me a headache.

I made it to the airport in record time to see her standing waiting for me. She didn't have any luggage so I knew she wouldn't be staying long. I got out the car to open the door for her to get in. She got in, sitting her purse on her lap before putting her seatbelt on. My mother was a beautiful woman with such an evil spirit. She was a green-eyed monster. Standing at 5'4 with long blonde hair and the complexion of maple syrup, my mother was a baddie. From the outside looking in, she was a beautiful stallion that could have any man she wanted, until she got him and he crossed her. That's when I stepped in take over. She could talk any nigga out his life. That proved to be true with my father and me. She talked me into taking my father's life, and that's something I'd never forgive her for. I still saw that nigga's face in my dreams. I was still fighting demons that no one but God could help me with.

I hit the highway back to my crib to talk to her. Once we were inside, I sat on the sofa, undid my tie, and took off my jacket. She sat on the table near me, and I looked at her. She had no mercy for the human life, and it was starting to show. I lost count of how many people I'd killed because of her. The funny thing was, I looked like her the most. I had her green eyes and her skin color. I hated to look in the mirror. I hated the reflection of the man I had become, the families I'd broken without their knowledge just because my mother said so. The hate that lived inside of me every time I took I took a life. She had no idea because she never took the time to ask me how I felt about the shit. She could have chosen her other two sons to carry this burden but instead, she chose me to get the blood on my hands. She loved each of us the same. She made sure we had something to fall back on when this illegal shit ran dry. That's the only thing I commend her and my father for. I leaned back on the couch and looked at her.

"To what do I owe this visit, Mother?" I asked her, and she reached in her purse and handed me a picture. I looked at it and it was a picture of a man I'd never seen before, but he looked familiar. Something about his eyes were familiar. I turned the picture over and there was an address written on the back of it.

"I got four hittas blending in down here, and I want this a clean kill. Only him, because he has a family. I don't want them hurt," she said, and I raised my eyebrow. Maybe she did have feelings inside that black heart of hers.

"I want them to suffer while they live without him," she said, looking into my eyes.

"Who the fuck is this and why do you want him killed? Is this why you sent me to New Orleans?" I asked her, because Khamakazee left to go back to Georgia because his wife threatened to leave him for not taking her with him. We had been telling him to bring her, but he didn't think we would be long, so it was like a business trip. He should have known if Khaya sent us somewhere then it would be for a long time.

"This one is personal," was all she offered, and it pissed me off.

"Killing my fucking father was personal, so what's personal about this nigga that you wanna kill him but spare his family?" I asked her, and she put her head down.

"Look, I give the fucking orders Khaza, so don't question me about who gets to live and who gets to die," she told me before standing from the table over me. "Let's not forget, everyone is replaceable," she said, and I took that as a fucking threat.

"Nah, that's where the fuck you wrong at. I can replace you, but you will never find a nigga to fill my shoes," I told her, and she piped down. Khaya thought everybody was scared of her, but I wasn't. If I could torture my fucking father, she would never be spared.

"Okay, you win, my love muffin. I need this done in 48 hours, and don't worry about bringing me back to the airport. I have a ride," she said, putting on her oversized Gucci shades. "And don't tell Khazeem I was here because I'll be back sooner than later. This wasn't a social visit." She kissed my cheek before strutting out of my home like she was the baddest bitch alive. I looked down at the picture and really stared at it. The man looked innocent, but his eyes told a story. I wondered if Khaya fucked him before and he fucked her over. I couldn't stare at it too long because I needed to change my clothes and head over to Khazeem's house so we could figure out a way I could get back into Ye's good graces.

I used my key to get into Khazeem's home and found him on the sofa playing the game, smoking a blunt. I flopped down next to him and took the blunt from him and smoked.

"What's up nigga, why you looking like a sad puppy, and what the fuck did you do to Ye? Because Muni and Nay ready to bang, nigga. You got Nay coming at me sideways while I was knee deep in the pussy like I knew what was going on. She said Ye was crying and shit. What the fuck did you do to that girl?" he asked me, never taking his eyes off the game. I didn't answer because I didn't know where to start. He paused the game, giving me his undivided attention.

"She a virgin, nigga, and I couldn't fuck with it so I put her out the house," I summed it up for him, because he didn't need all the details. He looked at me wide eyed.

"Nigga, you put her out or she left?" he asked me to be sure.

"I didn't know how to express myself, so when she said it I lost it and put her out. She left her phone at the house and shit, so I can't even call to apologize," I told him, and he laughed.

"Nigga, that's not funny. I need to fix this shit because I want her. I don't want no other nigga to have her," I told him honestly. My brothers were the only two people that knew how I disposed of women after fucking them. Ye was different. She gave me a different feeling, and I didn't know how to accept it.

"Do you really want to fix it though? You really trying to fuck with Ye like that?" he asked me.

"Yeah, I want her to teach me how to love her so I can do it right," I told him.

"Well, that's some shit that you need to be telling her, not me," he said, and I shrugged my shoulders.

"Nigga, don't you think if I knew how to get in touch with her that I would?" I asked him. "Call Nay for me," I asked, and he looked at me like I'd sprouted two heads. He shook his head and reached inside his pocket for his phone. He dialed her number and put it on speaker. She answered on the second ring.

"Hey bae, what's up? What you doing?" she answered the phone, and I could tell she was smiling.

"Hey babes, I need a favor. If you do this for me, I'll get you that Fendi bag with the matching slippers that you wanted," he tried to talk her into it.

"What's the favor, Khazeem?" she asked. "And if Khaza is involved and by you, tell that nigga I'mma beat the fuck outta him for hurting my friend. That shit different when you feel rejected," she said, and I felt hat shit in my soul.

"I need you to help my brother out with Ye because he over here losing it." Khazeem was laying it on a little too thick.

"As he should fucking be, because my friend was over here crying, all depressed and shit over his ass," she said in the phone like I couldn't hear her. I took the phone from him and off speaker.

"Look, I know I fucked up with her Nay, but that was a first for me and I didn't know how to express that to her. I reacted without thought and fucked up, but I'm trying make it right," I told her, meaning every word that came out my mouth.

"Since you sound like a wounded fucking puppy, I'll help you. I'm trying to get her out the house to go to the Lil' Weezyana Fest. Just so you know, it's the little things that you do for Yhen-tal. She's not materialistic and she loves flowers. Nigga, you better beg like Keith Sweat. Nah give my man his phone back," she told me, and I was happy she was going to help me. I gave him the phone back but put it on speaker.

"Khazeem, for that favor you can throw in the Fendi wallet and oversized shades, and we have a deal," she said.

"I got you," he told her, and they disconnected the phone.

"Nigga, you are paying for half of that shit," he said, laughing.

"Nigga, I'll pay for all of it to get back to Ye," I told him and stood to get something to drink.

"You got something to wear to the concert?" I asked Khazeem, because all this nigga wore were basketball shorts and t-shirts.

"Nigga, don't worry about me. You need to get you together and be ready to get your woman back," he said, and I knew what I had to do.

"I'm about to head out and put some shit in motion for Ye," I told him, grabbing my keys and heading to the door.

"Nigga, you better buy her a fucking unicorn. Shit'll blow her mind," he said, and I laughed. Nah, I had something better than a unicorn for her.

I still had two hours to get shit together, so I went to the flower shop to get rainbow-colored roses. I ordered every dozen they had. I went home and pulled my clothes out that I was wearing for the concert. A pair of Givenchy jeans and matching tee with a pair of black and white J's. I had it laid out on the sofa. I had the man deliver twenty dozen of those roses to my penthouse. I paid the housekeeper to decorate the room for me while I was gone. I wanted her to put the rose petals trailing from the front door to the bed. I had my personal shopper send over everything he could find that was Gucci. I also had her diamond and ruby bracelet sitting in the middle of the bed, and I also gave the lady twenty bands that had only hundreds in it. I told her to make a heart shape on the bed with that money. I had the chef for the building come in and cook lamb chops with loaded mash potatoes with a big bottle of D'ussé in case she was hungry. The candles were on the table, and I left them to it as I got dressed and went back by Khazeem's house. We were driving separate cars so that when I left I didn't have to worry about who was riding with who. I was going to make this a night that Yhental would never forget for years to come.

Yhental

"Bitch, you better get yo' whining ass up and get dressed before we are late for the concert," I heard Nay say as she walked in with bags from every store in the mall.

"I told you I wasn't going to that shit." I put the cover back over my head to lay down. After that shit with Khaza, I didn't want to go anywhere. Now I saw why my parents wanted me locked up in the house, and for once, I was enjoying it.

"Bitch, I walked through the mall for four hours looking for something that would fit yo' wide ass hips, so you gon' get up and put that shit on so we can pregame before we get to the concert." She threw the bags on the bed and pulled my cover back then sat on the bed near me. "Listen friend, this some real shit. People don't give a fuck about how you live your life unless you're miserable because misery loves company, but that's up to you. Khazeem makes me feel like I'm the only girl in his world and I am living in that moment until something changes, if it will ever change. Live yo' best life and worry about the other shit later because you only get one chance to do it. Fuck the people who don't like it and love the ones who do. Khaza made a mistake, but that's what niggas do. At least you didn't fuck him, but I know he is a good dude and he likes you. All I'm saying is give him another chance to show you what his mouth couldn't tell you in that moment, and I promise you won't regret it," she said like she knew something I didn't.

"Bitch, what did you do?" I asked her with a side eye.

"I didn't do shit. I'm just giving yo' ass some advice that you should take," she told me and got off the bed.

I knew she was only trying to make sure I was straight, and I loved her for that, but I couldn't risk going to the concert and seeing Khaza, or even worse, seeing him with another woman. That would break me, and I would end up in jail. What Khaza did to me that night fucked with my self-esteem, and I wasn't ready to face him. Everybody who was somebody was going to be at this concert, so I knew he was going to be there. I watched as she went in each bag and grabbed an item. She laid the shorts that were gon' barely cover my ass out on the bed with and diamond baby doll crop top with diamond sandals. This bitch must have thought I was the diamond princess because that was all I wore when she picked it out. On the other side of the bed was her black shorts, but she had a black blazer top that barely covered her breasts with a pair of sandals.

"It's a black out, bitch! We 'bout to turn the fuck up. Now get up and get dressed," she told me, and I dragged myself out the bed to the shower. I ran the water as hot as I could take it before taking my clothes off and getting in. I didn't want my hair straight, so I let the water hit it to make it curly. I was going for the Janet Jackson hair tonight. I got out the shower, wrapping the towel around my body and walking back to the room. Nay went in behind me to take her shower, and I sat at my vanity table. I wasn't wearing makeup tonight, only matte black lipstick. I grabbed my vanilla body lotion and lotioned my body before getting dressed. I looked at my ass in the shorts and knew I was going to regret wearing them because they would draw too much unwanted attention. I put my shirt on and slid my feet in my sandals. I grabbed my Apple watch from my dresser and slid it on my wrist. I sat on the bed to wait for Nay to get out the shower and get dressed.

After another hour of waiting for her, we were ready to go to the concert. I'd only heard stories about it but never actually went to it, so I was hyped to go. My father offered to let me drive his truck, but we declined, opting to grab an Uber instead. We stood in front the house facing a blunt and taking shots until the Uber showed up. We hopped in and smiled at each other, me more so wondering what the night would bring. I was glad that I had smoked that blunt because if not, my nerves would have been on edge when we pulled up. There were so many people out there waiting for Lil Wayne that we looked like dots. Everybody was taller than us, but we had exclusive passes thanks to my daddy and his connections. We walked right past the line and into the concert, taking our seats damn near to the stage. There were other people performing and a few surprise guests, and I hoped one of them was Nicki Minaj because I loved her. The performers had started, and we were two hours in when I wanted a drink.

"Where can I get a drink?" I asked Nay as she bobbed her head to the music.

"Over there, do you want me to come with you?" she asked me, and I shook my head no because it wasn't that far. I walked away and went to the bar and ordered me and Nay a Long Island iced tea. After paying for them and the bartender handing them to me, I walked back to where Nay was and handed her a drink.

"Come on, let's toast to the fun we are having and the fun that's about to come." We clinked our glasses, and she winked her eye at me because I didn't know what the fuck she was talking about. Nay could be really slick with shit, and I wouldn't find out until it was too late. We were dancing to the music until the DJ announced that Nicki Minaj was about to come to the stage. The audience went wild, and I was screaming right along with them. She walked out on the stage rapping my favorite song.

It was back in '07, did a couple of tapes

Did a couple DVDs, made a couple mistakes
Didn't know what I was doing, but I put on a cape
Now it's, "Which world tour should I go on today?"
See, you told me I would lose, but I won
I might cop a million Jimmy Choos just for fun
'Cause bitches couldn't take what was in me, Australia, Sydney
Might run up in Disney, out in LA with Lindsay
Got the eye of the tiger, the Lion of Judah
Now it's me and my time, it's just me in my prime
Everything I tried to teach 'em, they gon' see it in time
Tell 'em bitches get a stick, I'm done leadin' the blind
Got two shows tonight, that's Brooklyn and Dallas
Then a private party at the Buckingham Palace
Which means I gotta fly like a movie, no commercial
That's Young Money, Cash Money, yeah, I'm Universa*l*

I sang along with her as I rocked from side to side with the wind blowing in my hair. A bitch couldn't tell me I wasn't her twin. I loved everything about her from her style to how she was killing the music industry. I rocked my hips to the beat with my hands in the air, until I felt a hand wrapping around my waist from behind. I knew I had been drinking and smoking, but I knew Polo cologne and who wore it. I looked to my right and saw Nay kissing her man, not paying me any attention.

"I'm sorry," I heard him whisper in my ear, and I wanted to turn around and slap him but I had to think about where we were. I turned around and looked at him with evil eyes.

"Yeah, you are fucking sorry," I yelled over the music before running off. Nay tried to grab my arm, but I yanked away from her before the tears came. I knew Khaza was gon' be here, but I didn't think I would actually see him. I ran through the hallway that led to the bathroom, and he caught my arm, pushing me against the wall. He held my hands above my head with one of his hand and put the other around my waist. He pushed his body against mine, making me stand still. I tried to push him off me but he wouldn't budge.

"I'm sorry, I'm sorry, please, I'm sorry," he said into my neck as he kissed me there with every word.

"Please forgive me. Give me another chance because I didn't know what to do with the first one," he whispered in my ear, and I felt my heart melting away at his advances. His eyes met mine, and I got lost in his hues of green. We stared at each other before he kissed my lips hard and slow. I didn't give in easy, but when his tongue slithered in my mouth all bets were off. I couldn't resist his kisses. They set my soul free and the thought of another bitch getting them sent me into a fit of rage. I pulled away from him.

"You been giving bitches my kisses?" I asked him.

"Fuck no. I don't know nobody down here," he told me. "I only got eyes for you," he said and kissed me again. This time with more intensity. He grabbed the back of my head to deepen the kiss. I grabbed his ears, damn near ripping them off.

"Come with me, please," he begged with his mouth and eyes. I wanted to stay at the concert, but I wanted to go with him more. I walked away from him and went back to Nay.

"Bye bitch, thank me later." She kissed my cheek and I grabbed Khaza's hand to lead the way.

Once we got into his car, we headed in the direction of his penthouse. His hand was on my thigh the entire ride. When we went into the garage my body tensed and he felt it. Flashbacks of the last time I was there ran through my mind.

"Not this time," he said, kissing my cheek before parking the car and coming around to my side. I stepped out the car and he trapped me between him and the car. We were forehead to forehead.

"I only pushed you away because I was dealing wit' some shit on my end, but I promise if you show me how to love you, I'll never love another." He looked in my eyes before kissing my lips. I wanted to cry but I held it because I was a big girl. He pulled me from the car before closing the door and hitting the alarm, and we went to the elevator. He kissed and licked everywhere he could on the ride to the 10th floor. I couldn't wait until we got to the mile high club. The elevator doors opened and we walked down the short hallway to his penthouse. He unlocked the door and opened it for me to go in first.

"Oh my god, Khaza." My hands went to my mouth as the tears start to come. My favorite flowers were all over the room. I walked further into the room, following the rose petals that led to a table set for dinner for two, but I wasn't thinking about food. My clit was thumping. I wanted him in the worst way. He held my waist as I followed the second trail to the bedroom, and there were more rainbow roses everywhere. I looked at the bed and there was a heart shape full of hundred-dollar bills surrounding it. I turned to him and jumped in his arms because I wasn't expecting this at all.

"My crybaby," he whispered in my hair as I started to pull his shirt off of him. There was no way he was denying me tonight.

I pushed him on the bed, taking his shirt off. He kissed and sucked my belly button and hips as he slid my shorts and shirt off. I pulled his jeans and boxers down and he stood to take the rest off. I looked at his dick as it sprang in the air. I pushed him back on the bed, on top of the money, and fell to my knees. His hand ran through my hair as I looked into his green eyes.

"Show me," I told him, and he nodded his head.

"Wet ya mouth, bae." I did as he said.

"Just watch ya teeth and freestyle it to your favorite beat," he said, and I sucked his mushroom tip. I slid my mouth up and down his shaft at a slow pace. I had to relax my muscles to take him all the way in.

"Fuck," he groaned out, and I moaned, bobbing my head up and down faster and faster until his thighs tensed. He pulled me up by my hair and sloppily kissed me.

"I want to nut in that pussy, not in yo' mouth, pretty girl," he said, pulling me to my feet. We switched positions with me laying on top of the money. He crawled between my legs while whispering, "My bitch bad looking like a bag of money." He started with my lips before making his way to my breasts. After giving them much-needed attention, he was back at my mouth. I felt his dick poking at my entrance, and my body tensed.

"We don't have to do this right now, Ye," he whispered against my lips. I reached between us, bringing his head back to my opening.

"I want it Khaza, please," I begged for it. He pushed in and out, making me wetter and wetter, until he was all the way in. I screamed and bit into his shoulder to numb the pain. That pain turned into pleasure as he rocked inside of me.

"Fuck me back, pretty girl," he said, and I started to move my hips. He stuck his tongue out and I sucked on it for dear life.

"Umm, fuck." I watched his face turn into a scowl as we moved against each other. He raised up, putting weight on his arms to look at our connection.

"Man, look how powerful this pussy is gripping my shit," he said, pulling all the way out and easing back in. "You gon' have a nigga doing life behind this pussy. Please don't share it," he whispered against my lips.

"I promise, I won't," I told him, and I felt his dick jump inside of me. My clit jumped, and a heat wave came over my body. My legs vibrated and liquid gushed out of me onto his shaft. He flipped my body over and arched my back before sliding in. This shit had to be heaven because that's what I felt as he slowly pumped in and out of me until he couldn't take it anymore and nutted inside of me. I didn't even think about using a condom. He fell to the side of me on his back, and I fell on him.

"There's so much more I want to teach you, but in time you'll know everything you need to know," he said before we both drifted off into a peaceful slumber.

I jumped out my sleep to find Khaza on his back knocked out. I got out the bed to look for my phone to call Nay to come get me. I still had to respect my parents' home. After her reply, I put my clothes on and went to his side of the bed.

"Bae, I gotta go, Nay outside," I told him, and he lifted his head a little.

"Where you going? What about all the stuff I got you?" he asked, still half sleep.

"I'm coming back by you tonight. I gotta go home and get some clothes," I told him before kissing his lips.

"Take the key on the counter to let your yourself in just in case I'm not here." I grabbed the key walked down to Nay's awaiting car with a slight bow in my legs.

Khaza

After the night I had with Yhental, I felt like a new man, but I still had to carry out this mission for my mother. I wanted to tell Ye so much, but I couldn't because she wanted the dick. After I did this kill, I would come back to her and tell her everything about me. Right now, I had to get ready for work. I stepped into my closet and grabbed my black thermal and hoodie with my bulletproof vest. I out on my black Timbs and jeans before going under my bed and grabbing my rifle. I knew the niggas were downstairs waiting on me, but I had to get my mind right. All images and feelings for Yhental had to go on the back burner because Kellz was currently taking over. He was my alter ego when I went on a job, but I would turn back to Khaza when I was back in her arms. I hated this shit, but it had to be down. I took the fire escape down to the main floor and slid out the side door with ease. I hopped in the car with three of Khaya's hittas seated around me, waiting on me to speak. Khaya wasn't slick. She sent these niggas to make sure they watched me kill whoever this nigga was. She said it was a clean kill, so no torturing required, although that was my favorite part.

"There are four guards sitting on the perimeter of the house. I need two snipers on top to take them out and the other two come with me. No one dies but the target. I don't give a fuck if you see a family member, just walk the fuck away," I told them, and they all nodded in agreement. "I will deliver the kill shot. I just need y'all to cover me," I told them, and I hit the back seat, signaling the driver to pull off.

When we pulled up on side of the gate, I told him to kill the lights. We hopped out and everybody went their separate ways. This should be no more than a 20-minute job because we were going through the front door. We waited to hear the shots before we made our move.

Pew pew pew pew

That was our signal to slowly go inside the house and to the master suite. We moved in silence through the house and up the stairs. We checked the rooms until we found the right one. We moved in the room silently, and the two men I had with me stood by the door. I looked down at this man and his wife as they slept. He didn't even know what was coming to him. I screwed the silencer on and sent two shots to the dome, and we walked back into the hallway.

Crashhhhhh

The sound of glass hitting the floor caused me to turn around. I looked into the eyes of the one person whose heart I didn't want to break, but the deed was already done. One hitta pulled his gun, but I pushed it away.

"Fuck no, we got who we came for," I spoke through my clown mask as I made eye contact with Yhental. I had just killed her and she didn't know, or did she?

"Oh my god, what have you done?!" she screamed to the top of her lungs while grabbing her phone. She didn't know it was me, and I'd never forget the look on her face. I grabbed the two niggas as we jumped over the railing and landed on our feet. I thought she was calling the police, but she wasn't. As we walked out the door like the killers we were, I stopped dead in my tracks when I heard her angelic voice say, “Teedy Nobby, where my uncle Magnolia at?! Somebody just shot my daddy,” she screamed in the phone, and I knew a war was coming.

Awwwwwww, to be continued...

Also By Miss. Jazzie

When The Side B*tch Understands The Assignment 2

The Wife Of A Certified Henchman 3

The Wife Of A Certified Henchman 2

When The Side B*tch Understands The Assignment

The Wife Of A Certified Henchman

Magnolia & Dior 2: A Hood Love Story

Magnolia & Dior: A Hood Love Story

Married To The Don Of New Orleans

Married To The Don Of New Orleans 2

Married To The Don Of New Orleans 3

A Nolia Boss Saved Me

A Nolia Boss Saved Me 2

A Nolia Boss Saved Me 3

Made in United States
Orlando, FL
13 November 2022